This copy of

THE RIDDLE OF THE FROZEN FOUNTAIN
by Carolyn Keene

belongs to

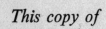

Donna M. Noble

9 Old Evanton Road

Carolyn Keene

The Riddle of the Frozen Fountain

SPARROW
BOOKS

A Sparrow Book
Published by Arrow Books Limited
3 Fitzroy Square, London W1P 6JD

An imprint of the Hutchinson Publishing Group

London Melbourne Sydney Auckland
Wellington Johannesburg and agencies
throughout the world

First published in Great Britain 1981
© Grosset & Dunlap Inc. 1964, 1972

This book is sold subject to the condition that
it shall not, by way of trade or otherwise, be
lent, resold, hired out, or otherwise circulated
without the publisher's prior consent in any
form of binding or cover other than that in
which it is published and without a similar condition including this condition being imposed
on the subsequent purchaser

Made and printed in Great Britain
by The Anchor Press Ltd
Tiptree, Essex

ISBN 0 09 926430 7

CONTENTS

CHAPTER I

Nymphs in the Storm

"THIS is a real blizzard!" gasped Louise Dana to her sister Jean.

"And this wind! I can hardly see a thing!"

The two attractive girls were plowing their way through a raging snowstorm to get back to Starhurst School where they were enrolled as boarding students. The storm had come up suddenly and was quickly adding inches to the already deep snow.

"I'm half frozen!" said Jean, as she slid sideways on some hidden ice and nearly fell. "Our hiking adventure through the woods this afternoon was fun at first, but now it's positively dangerous!"

The sisters could hardly see which way to go, but presently Jean noticed part of a hedge and said, "We're almost at the vacant old Price homestead. Let's take shelter there."

Louise, dark-haired and brown-eyed, was seventeen, a year older than her sister, and she was not so impulsive. "It's probably locked," she said dubiously, "and we shouldn't break in."

Jean, her teeth chattering, remarked, "It's better than freezing to death!"

"I guess you're right. Let's go!"

The girls changed their course a bit and soon came to a snow-covered path. It led through a large garden to the old Price house, which sat far back from the street. In the center of the garden stood a graceful bronze fountain, about six feet high. Above its basin, which was half-filled with leaves and ice, was a slender stem. Circling this, near the top, were a group of dancing nymphs, now covered with ice and snow.

The Danas, despite their desire to get indoors, paused a few moments to admire the fountain. "It's beautiful," said Louise, a dreamy look in her dark eyes. "I don't wonder Professor Crandall wanted to buy it."

Professor Crandall was the husband of Starhurst's headmistress. He taught history and philosophy at the school. Although Louise and Jean were often amused by his absent-mindedness, they were very fond of him.

Blond, blue-eyed Jean shivered. "N-nothing looks b-beautiful to me right now! Come on. Let's get out of this biting wind!"

The girls pushed on toward the house. Just before reaching it, Louise exclaimed, "Look, Jean! There's a light in one of the second-floor rooms!

That's strange. The house is supposed to be empty."

"Maybe somebody else went in there to take shelter."

When the Danas reached the rambling three-story homestead, they went up the front porch steps and pounded on the door. There was no response.

"Whoever is inside doesn't want visitors," said Jean. "Well, I don't care! I'm going to get warm!"

"Probably no one is here. Whoever is in charge of the property may have left a light on by mistake," Louise suggested. "Let's walk around the house and see if we can find an unlocked window."

It was difficult wading in the deep snow, and to the sisters' dismay, not one window was unlocked.

"I guess we'll *have* to break in," said Jean.

"All right," Louise assented. "We'll break a pane in a porch window and slip the catch. We can pay for the damage later."

The words were scarcely out of her mouth when Jean climbed the porch steps and thrust her heavily gloved hand through one of the panes. The lock was opened, the window lifted, and the sisters stepped over the sill. They closed the window, then looked around. Evidently they were in the living room. It was completely bare, but to the girls' delight they discovered logs laid in the large stone fireplace.

"We're really in luck," said Jean.

On the mantel lay a packet of matches. Louise quickly lighted the newspaper crumpled under the kindling and logs, and within minutes there was a roaring blaze.

Jean grinned. "I wonder how long it will take me to thaw out. I feel as if it would take—"

She stopped speaking and the sisters exchanged startled glances. From somewhere on the second floor they had heard a loud *thump*, as if something or somebody had fallen.

"That light *did* mean someone is here!" Louise exclaimed excitedly. "Let's see what happened."

The two girls dashed from the room out to a hallway and up the stairs to the second floor. They peered into the nearest bedroom, then the others. No one was there. Next, the girls searched all the closets. These also were empty.

Louise pressed a switch button on the wall. No lights came on. "Whoever was up here had a flashlight," she said.

"One thing is clear," said Jean. "He had no right in this place, or he wouldn't have avoided us."

Louise shrugged. "Perhaps he had a right to be here, but had some other reason for not wanting to meet us."

At the rear of the hall was an open door leading to a downward flight of steps. "Maybe he went this way," Jean remarked. "Let's go down and find out. I don't like playing hide-and-seek with some mysterious person in an old deserted house."

A sudden blast of icy air came up the stairway. "I think your mysterious person has gone out the back way and left the door open," said Louise.

The sisters dashed down the steps. Louise's assumption was correct. On the snowy back porch were footprints that led down the steps and off through the grounds.

"A man of medium height," stated Jean, gazing at the average-sized prints. Then she closed the self-locking door.

For a few minutes Louise and Jean had forgotten about being cold. Now they began to shiver and went to stand in front of the roaring fire to warm themselves. Finally, after the floor boards in front of the hearth had heated up, they seated themselves. The Danas discussed the man who had just left. What was his name? Why had he been there? What had dropped upstairs?

"Since he didn't break any windows or doors, he must have had a key," Louise surmised.

"It's my guess there's something fishy about the whole affair," Jean declared. "No one in his right mind would go out in a blizzard with a chance to enjoy a nice cozy fireplace."

Louise sighed. "I wonder how long we'll have to stay. If this snow keeps on, we'll have a hard time getting back to school in time for dinner."

Then another thought came to Louise. "This old homestead faces a street. We'd better return that way instead of through the woods."

She looked out a window. The storm showed no signs of abating. The wind whistled, and rattled the old windowpanes. Tree limbs creaked and one brushed eerily against the house.

"This is really weird," said Jean. "A house has been vacant for a long time, and yet there were logs laid in this fireplace." Suddenly she got up and walked over to a corner where there was a small pile of newspapers. As she crumpled one sheet to stuff it into the broken windowpane, she glanced at the date.

"This paper isn't very old," she said. "Only two weeks!"

Louise smiled. "Another mystery." Then she changed the subject. "By the looks of that icy fountain in the garden, it'll be a long time before Professor Crandall can move it to the school grounds. But what a nice addition for Starhurst!"

"Didn't the professor say the fountain had been designed by the famous Italian sculptor, Benvenuto Cellini?"

"It's supposed to be," her sister replied.

The girls kept an anxious eye on the storm. Finally, an hour later, the wind died down and the snow ceased. Louise and Jean decided to set off for Starhurst. By this time the fire was burning low and was easily extinguished with several handfuls of snow.

"Let's go home through the woods," Jean suggested. "It won't be so bad now that the snow's stopped. I'd like to see where that strange intruder went. Besides, it's a short cut to school."

Louise nodded. They closed the back door and set off without disturbing the man's footprints. To their surprise, the sisters found that he had not walked very far. Tire tracks in a clearing indicated a car had been parked there. "The mystery man drove away," Louise observed. The tracks went directly through a clearing in the woods which led to a back road.

Louise and Jean turned in the other direction and trekked on among the trees. At the far side of the woods a slope led down to a pond on the Starhurst grounds. Near the main building which housed offices, classrooms, and dormitories they noticed a small snow figure some of the students apparently had made. It was already covered with ice.

The Danas hurried into the basement, where they removed their boots and lined them up near those of other students. Then the sisters climbed a rear stairway to the second floor.

"Louise! Jean!" called a pretty girl, hurrying toward the sisters. "Where *have* you been? Everybody has been frantic about you!"

The speaker was slim, dark-haired Evelyn Starr, whose family had originally owned the estate which later had been converted into a school.

"Tell you at supper," said Jean. "Right now I'm headed for a hot bath!"

Evelyn giggled. "Not yet."

"Why?" Louise asked.

"Because Professor Crandall sent a message and said he wanted to see you two the minute you returned."

The Danas went down the front stairway and walked directly to the suite occupied by Professor and Mrs. Crandall. The bespectacled, grey-haired professor answered their knock.

"Come in, come in!" he said excitedly. "I have a mystery for you girls to solve. But no publicity, and no police, please." He pulled a paper from his coat pocket and handed it to Louise. "This is a threatening note which I received today!"

CHAPTER II

Mystery Queen

BEFORE Louise and Jean had a chance to read the threatening note, the door opened and Mrs. Crandall came in. She was a tall, stern-looking woman, who, though kind and understanding, ruled Starhurst School with a firm hand.

She smiled at the Danas, saying, "Good evening, girls." Then her face clouded. "That note is an outrage!"

The Danas told her that they had not yet read it, but did so at once. The hand-printed words gave them a distinct shock. The message was:

DO NOT DISTURB FOUNTAIN OR
YOU WILL BE IN GREAT DANGER.

"This *is* a sinister warning," Louise commented. "Professor Crandall, when did you receive it?"

"In the afternoon mail." He produced the envelope, which bore the same printing as the note.

"There's no clue to the sender," Jean spoke up, "except that the letter was mailed right here in Penfield."

Professor Crandall looked angry. "I paid for the Cellini fountain with the understanding that I would not have to move it until the weather was better. The fountain is embedded in concrete, and that, together with deep snow and frozen ground, makes it difficult and expensive to take it from the Price homestead just now."

The professor went on to say that moreover he would have to find a feasible spot in which to place the fountain. "I hope to locate a spring on the grounds. If this is not possible, the water will have to be piped, and the expense will be heavy."

Louise and Jean did not comment, but they felt that despite the trouble involved, the fountain should be removed from the homestead property as soon as possible. At least it could be stored in a safe place until a proper location was found.

The girls studied the warning. They noticed that it was printed in very dark capital letters. Louise ventured an opinion. "I believe this is the work of a bold, aggressive, fearless man. Whoever printed the note has a strong, heavy touch."

Mrs. Crandall looked worried, but her husband unexpectedly smiled. "It's possible someone is trying to bluff us."

"I'm not so sure of that." The headmistress's tone was serious.

Jean did not take sides in these divergent opinions. Instead, she told the Crandalls about the strange experience she and Louise had had at the Price homestead and about the man who had been upstairs and sneaked out without revealing his identity. "Maybe he is the same person who wrote this note."

The headmistress's forehead creased into a deep frown. "I cannot blame you girls for taking shelter against the storm, but you might have found yourselves in great danger.' Please do not go into the house again unaccompanied."

The Danas promised, then continued to study the note. Presently Louise held the sheet sideways to the lamplight. "Have you a magnifying glass?" she asked the Crandalls.

The professor took one from a desk drawer and Louise scrutinized the sheet. "Here's something that may be a clue," she said. "See these indentations in the paper? I believe the person who wrote the warning was wearing a ring on his little finger."

The Crandalls looked startled and the headmistress said, "I know you girls are excellent sleuths, but please explain your deduction."

"Let me show you," Louise said. She laid the paper on the table. "Watch the little finger of my right hand."

As she moved her hand back and forth over the sheet, as if writing, the others could see how she was tracing the almost invisible zigzag lines.

"Very clever!" said Professor Crandall. "Well, I have given you girls the assignment of finding the sender of this warning note. I hope you do it soon. I am concerned about that valuable fountain."

Both Louise and Jean welcomed the challenge. In their recent adventure, *Mystery of the Stone Tiger*, the Danas had been successful in tracking down a black-robed ghost who was terrifying the people in their home town. Now they were eager to tackle this new mystery.

Before leaving the Crandalls' apartment, the girls asked who was in charge of the Price homestead. They learned that Mr. Ralph Black, a Penfield estate agent, had the property listed for sale and was taking care of both the old house and the grounds.

"He is the one who obtained permission from the heirs of the deceased owner to sell me the fountain," Professor Crandall explained.

Louise said, "I'll phone Mr. Black and tell him about the broken window. If we may, Jean and I would like to go down to his office and pay for it."

The headmistress nodded and then said the girls had better hurry to get ready for dinner. They hastened off. Louise stopped long enough to phone Mr. Black, who requested that the girls see him Monday, since he would be away for the week end.

Louise and Jean found Evelyn Starr waiting upstairs. "Why did Professor Crandall want to see you?" she asked.

"Come into our rooms while we change," said Jean, "and we'll tell you all about it."

Evelyn followed the girls into their two-room suite. As the Danas quickly freshened up and put on simple wool dresses, they told Evelyn about their new assignment as amateur detectives. "Professor Crandall doesn't want the police informed, and no publicity," said Louise, "so we'll have to keep this to ourselves. We'll let Doris in on our secret, but no one else."

Doris Harland was another close friend of the Danas and had shared several adventures with them. A few minutes later Doris came into the room. She was a very pretty girl, blond and blue-eyed, with delicate features.

When Doris heard the story, she became a little alarmed. "I don't like the sound of that spooky old mansion. I'm glad Mrs. Crandall made you promise not to go there alone again."

Jean laughed. "Okay, Doris, we'll take you along to meet the ghost."

Doris looked at her friend out of the corner of her eye. She was a good sport, but did not react to frightening situations as fearlessly as the Danas or Evelyn. Nevertheless, she had a quick retort.

"If you'll promise me he'll be tall, dark, and handsome, I'll be glad to meet your ghost!"

Evelyn chuckled. "Can't you just see Doris dating a tall, dark, and handsome ghost!"

The dinner gong rang, and the four girls started down the stairs. On the way they met Lettie Briggs and her friend Ina Mason. Ina, a rather sullen person, was known as Lettie's shadow. Lettie herself was called "the pest" by many of the other students. This tall, sharp-featured girl was disliked because of her petulance and constant bragging. She was particularly envious of the Danas' popularity.

"Where were you this afternoon, Louise and Jean?" she asked loudly. "You had your nerve getting everyone in a dither thinking you got lost in the storm."

"Are you disappointed?" Jean queried impishly. "As a matter of fact, we were so frozen a couple of children thought we were walking icicles!"

Other students on their way to dinner, hearing the remark, burst into laughter but Lettie did not even smile.

Just before dessert was served, Mrs. Crandall arose and said she had an announcement of interest to make. A skating competition and exhibition would be held on the school pond a week from the next day.

"Starhurst is inviting the boys of Walton Academy to be our guests for that week end, and participate in the events." She smiled. "Many of you have friends at Walton, and I am sure you will be happy to skate with them."

Louise turned around and looked at her sister. Two boys whom they enjoyed dating attended Walton. Louise's friend was Ken Scott, and Chris Barton was always Jean's partner. All were excellent skaters. The sisters exchanged pleased grins.

Mrs. Crandall went on, "Several prizes will be given and a queen and escort will be chosen from among the contestants."

The girls clapped and began to talk animatedly about the forthcoming events. When dinner was over, Lettie caught up with Louise. The unpleasant girl tossed her head, and gave Louise a supercilious look. "I suppose," said Lettie, "you think you and Ken will be chosen queen and escort!"

Without waiting for a reply, she stalked from the room. Louise was wondering what Lettie hoped to gain by such sarcasm when Jean caught up to her sister. "Isn't the news exciting!" Jean said.

Louise nodded. "Pretty wonderful. Say, Jean, this is the evening we have to go to the advanced English class session in the library."

A few students at Starhurst had been selected to try out a group study experiment. The Danas were among them and hurried to the library.

Two hours later they were dismissed. Wearily they climbed the stairs to their suite. Louise entered and snapped on the light. She gasped and cried out, "Oh, no!"

Jean, who had paused in the hallway, rushed into the room. "What's the matter?" Then she saw what had startled her sister.

In the middle of Louise's bed stood the ice-covered snow figure they had seen on the lawn.

On it was a sign:

THE MYSTERY QUEEN

Jean roared with laughter. "It's not a snowman, but a snow woman!"

Louise did not think the situation so funny. The snow woman had started to melt. "Look! My bed is soaked and so is this rug in front of it! What a mess!"

Jean asked, "Have you any idea who put this here?"

"Yes, I have," said Louise.

CHAPTER III

Vanished Footprints

Under her breath Louise said, "I believe Lettie is responsible for this snow figure." She told Jean of the unpleasant girl's sarcastic remark.

"I'll bet you're right," Jean agreed. "But how are we going to prove it?"

Her sister shrugged and said, "First of all, let's get this melting snow woman out of here."

Together, the two girls endeavoured to lift the figure from the bed and pitch it out the window. Unfortunately it broke into three pieces, getting more of the room wet. Finally the Danas succeeded in throwing the chunks of snow out the window.

"I'll never be able to change my whole bed and undress before the lights-out bell," Louise wailed.

Nevertheless, she and Jean went to work on the soggy bedclothes. Spread, sheets, and blankets were hurriedly pulled off.

"Good night!" came Evelyn Starr's voice from the doorway. "What on earth is going on?"

The Danas turned to face their friend, clad in robe and pajamas. Ruefully they told the story of the snow woman, and of their suspicions as to the culprit.

"Oh, that Lettie!" Evelyn said in disgust. "Right now, I'll do what I can to help. There's not much time."

She ran to the linen closet and soon returned with extra supplies.

"Even the mattress is soaked!" Louise said woefully. "We can't replace that!"

"I have an idea," said Evelyn. "Marge Cooper down the hall is away for the night. We'll borrow her mattress."

She and Jean rushed off to get it. They had just returned to the Dana suite when the lights-out bell sounded.

"Evelyn, you scoot," Louise advised. "Jean and I will just have to take our punishment for not being ready."

"Aren't you going to tell what happened?" Evelyn asked.

Louise shook her head. Then she grinned. "We'll get even some other way."

Miss Webster, a mathematics teacher, was monitor for the evening. She raised her eyebrows at the dishevelled condition of Louise's bedroom. "What happened?" she asked sternly.

"I'm sorry, Miss Webster," Louise replied. "We have a little problem here. That's why we're not ready for bed."

The teacher looked at both girls, but asked no further questions. She said, "You know what this means. I will recommend to Mrs. Crandall that both you girls spend two hours in the kitchen before dinner tomorrow—that is, unless you wish to plead your case."

"We have no excuse," Louise told her. "We'll take our punishment."

Miss Webster went on down the hall to inspect other rooms. The Danas quickly finished making Louise's bed, and a few minutes later tucked themselves under the covers.

The following morning, as the sisters were dressing, they discussed ways in which to trap Lettie into a confession. Jean prophesied that this would not be possible. "But maybe Ina will give the whole thing away."

The first clue came in mathematics class that morning. The instructor found Lettie totally unprepared. She had not done any part of her assigned homework.

"I couldn't help it," the girl said, rather defiantly. "I had a bad headache last night."

From across the room Evelyn Starr winked at Louise, and after class she whispered, "I'm sure Lettie is faking. When I saw her a couple of times last night, she didn't act as if she had a headache."

Just then Doris came up. "What's this, a secret conference?" she asked the three with a smile.

The Danas brought her up to date. Doris nodded knowingly. "I'm sure you're right about Lettie. While you two were in the library, I saw her and Ina sneaking along the hall with coats on. They were giggling. An hour later I saw them again. They were just scooting back into their room. Their hands were quite red. I'll bet it was from handling snow!"

Jean, Doris, and Evelyn moved off to another class. Louise had a free period and because she was on the honour roll was allowed to spend it in her room rather than with a group in the study hall. Lettie and Ina did not enjoy such a privilege, so Louise slipped into their room to look for any telltale evidence that the two girls had made the mystery snow woman.

On the radiator cover lay two pairs of very damp mittens!

"I know Lettie and Ina weren't outside this morning," Louise said to herself as she left the room.

The afternoon was taken up with sports, which were required of all students. This gave the Danas an opportunity to practise for the competition. Louise was a very graceful figure skater, while Jean enjoyed racing and ice hockey.

"This is fun," Jean remarked to Louise as they paused for breath. "But I wish we could do some sleuthing soon on the frozen fountain mystery. Professor Crandall expects us to solve it."

"I do too," said Louise. She smiled. "In the meantime, want to help me play a little joke on Lettie Briggs?"

"You bet I do! What?"

"I'll tell you when we get to the kitchen." Louise looked at her wristwatch. "Oh, we'd better leave right away!"

The sisters worked hard at the pre-dinner chores assigned them. It was not until they were helping to spoon the dessert into sherbert glasses that Louise whispered her plan to Jean.

"On top of this luscious fruit pudding goes a big dab of whipped cream. What say we give Lettie an extra amount, and in case she should find it too sweet, add a generous quantity of salt?"

Jean's eyes sparkled. "I'll get the salt," she offered. "We shan't be serving, so we'll have to put Lettie's name on her plate." She grinned as Louise pulled out a small piece of paper with Lettie's name on it from her apron pocket. "You think of everything, Sis!"

Soon the gong rang. The Danas removed their aprons and went into the dining room. That evening, under the rotation system, the sisters were sitting with Evelyn and Doris and whispered their secret to them. They in turn passed the word along to several other special friends.

When the dessert for Lettie's table was brought

in by a maid, Lettie looked a little surprised to find her name under the sherbert glass served to her. She looked very much pleased, however, upon noticing that she had a larger portion of whipped cream than anyone else.

As soon as Mrs. Crandall dipped her own spoon into the dessert, Lettie scooped up as much of hers as possible. Many eyes in the room were turned on her as the whipped cream disappeared into Lettie's mouth.

Suddenly a startled expression came over Lettie's face, then one of horror as she swallowed the salty concoction. A moment later she began to cough violently and stood up. With a black look directed toward the Danas, Lettie hurried from the dining room.

All the girls who knew the secret began to giggle. But when Mrs. Crandall looked at them, puzzled, they resumed eating their own desserts quietly.

Doris whispered to Louise, "Lettie knows you did it. I'm sure she'll try playing another trick on you. Watch your step!"

"That's right," said Evelyn. "Lettie never admits she has only been paid back. She's always intent on pulling another trick."

The following morning everyone attended Sunday church services. After midday dinner there was a musicale. The girls spent the rest of the day catching up on correspondence and homework.

Monday afternoon Louise and Jean went to the office of the agent, Mr. Black. After paying for the broken windowpane in the Price house, the Danas learned from the dark-haired, mustached man that a new pane would have to be put in at once because a down payment had been made on the property.

"Then the fountain will have to be removed immediately?" Louise asked him.

"Oh, there's no hurry," he said. "I have informed the new owners that the fountain was not included in the purchase."

Jean told him about the man who had been in the house the day the girls were there. "Perhaps he was the new owner," she added.

"No," the realtor replied. "The buyer has no keys yet." Suddenly Mr. Black frowned. "Did the place look as if anything had been stolen?" he queried.

Jean startled him by saying that there was nothing at all in the house.

"What!" he exclaimed. "The house contained valuable art objects which weren't included in the sale."

The Danas were startled. "We heard something heavy drop," Jean said. "That's the reason we went upstairs, but there was no one around and the rooms were empty."

Mr. Black looked intently at the girls. "You know, you two could be considered suspects."

Louise smiled. "In that case, Mr. Black, we never would have come to you."

"True." The agent said he would report the theft of the art objects to the police. "Can you girls tell me anything else?"

Louise mentioned the footprints leading from the back porch of the house to the spot from which the intruder had apparently driven away. Mr. Black thanked the girls for the information and turned to his telephone. The Danas stood up and said they must get back to school.

Just before dinnertime that evening Louise was summoned to the phone. The caller was Mr. Black and he had some amazing information. The police had just been to the Price homestead to investigate. The footprints of Louise and Jean were still visible, but there were no others. The police might question the girls later about the intruder they had heard.

When Louise reported this to Jean, her sister's eyes opened wide in astonishment. "But we distinctly saw the man's footprints," Jean declared.

"Of course we did," Louise agreed. "Let's ask Mrs. Crandall's permission to go over there early tomorrow morning before breakfast."

"Good idea. And let's take Evelyn and Doris with us."

Permission was granted and at six-thirty the next morning the four girls trekked through the woods. When they reached the frozen fountain, Evelyn and Doris exclaimed over its beauty.

Evelyn added, "This lovely piece will look even better on the Starhurst grounds."

The girls followed the snowy path which led to the house and immediately walked around to the back entrance. Louise and Jean stared in disbelief.

The mysterious man's footprints were indeed no longer there!

"We didn't just dream it!" Jean insisted.

Louise had noticed something unusual. She got down on her knees and looked across the snow at eye level.

"Girls!" she cried excitedly. "I have an idea about what happened!"

CHAPTER IV

Snowball Warning

LOUISE's three companions, curious, also stooped down for an eye level view of the snow. All admitted they could see nothing unusual.

Very carefully Louise began to scoop out snow from a certain spot. In a few minutes Jean, Doris, and Evelyn were startled to see the clear outline of a man's footprint below.

Jean's eyes were bright with excitement. "Now I see what you're driving at, Louise. You think someone deliberately filled up these footprints so they could not be investigated."

"Exactly," her sister replied. "Either the man himself backtracked, carrying a bucket of snow with him, or more likely a woman did it, using Jean's and my footprints to step in."

"It's a clever trick," Doris remarked. "That man obviously is afraid of being found out."

Evelyn continued to stare as Louise scooped out snow from several more of the mysterious stranger's prints. Finally she asked, "When do you figure these prints were filled in?"

"Soon after the man made them," Louise answered. "A crust has already formed on top of the snow, and on some of the prints you can hardly tell where the edge was."

Evelyn suggested that the police should be notified at once so they could investigate the newest clue promptly. At the moment the sole of the footprint was still hard and visible. "I'll run to a phone and call headquarters."

"Oh, would you?" said Louise. "That would be wonderful."

Evelyn hurried off down the front walk of the homestead. While she was gone, the other girls continued to uncover more of the hidden footprints.

"Guess we have enough," said Louise.

Next, they began looking for any other clues which the man, or any of his confederates, might have left. None came to light. As the threesome stood by some trees at the rear of the house, discussing the mystery, they were suddenly bombarded with a barrage of snowballs from the woods beyond.

"Ouch!" Louise winced as she received a stinging blow on her head.

Jean cried out as a hard one struck her arm, and both girls dodged behind trees to avoid serious injury.

Doris, farther away from a hiding place, found herself directly in the path of a rocketing snowball which hit her behind one ear. As the snowball disintegrated, the Danas were horrified to see a stone fall to the ground. Doris wavered uncertainly, clutching her head. The next instant she toppled over unconscious.

"Oh, Doris!" Louise cried out.

She and Jean, forgetting their own safety, dashed out to assist their friend. At the same moment, a large snowball smashed against the tree alongside Jean. As it did, a piece of paper which had been inside the snowball fluttered to the earth.

Jean paused a moment to pick it up. Five words, printed by hand in capital letters, stood out boldly. The message read:

GET OUT AND STAY OUT!

"Another warning!" Jean murmured.

As she ran to Doris's side, she glanced in the direction from which the snowballs had come. The attack had suddenly stopped. Jean could see no one.

Louise had already reached Doris, and was cradling the girl's head in her arms. "She's coming to," Louise reported in relief.

"Thank goodness!" said Jean, and showed her sister the note. As Louise gasped, Jean remarked, "I couldn't see who fired this."

Louise was furious. "What a vicious thing!" she burst out.

The words were hardly out of her mouth when the Danas saw Evelyn and two policemen making their way toward the homestead. Jean ran to meet them and explained about the snowball assault.

Evelyn grew pale. "How terrible!"

"I guess Doris has regained consciousness by this time," Jean reassured her.

Both policemen frowned. One of them, Officer Hodge, remarked that it was strange how the peaceful old homestead had suddenly become a place of mystery. He asked, "Do you think this was a prank played by one of your schoolmates?"

Jean thought of Lettie Briggs. Had she done this to get even with the Danas? The girl quickly decided Lettie would not be so mean as to throw a rock snowball at them.

"No, I don't think so," Jean replied. She now showed the men the footprints which Louise had uncovered and at once they began to take measurements and photographs.

By this time Louise, with Doris clinging to her arm, came up to the group. Jean and Evelyn asked solicitously how Doris felt.

"I'm all right except my head aches badly," she said. "I think I'll go back to school right now, and rest before classes start."

Officer Hodge turned to his companion. "Bill, suppose you drive this young lady to Starhurst, while I finish up the job here."

Evelyn offered to go along. Officer Bill Hamer

and the two girls went down the front walk to the street and got into the patrol car.

Officer Hodge now turned to Louise and said, "Uncovering these camouflaged footprints was a clever bit of detecting."

Louise blushed a little and said she hoped it would help to track down the person who apparently had stolen several valuable art objects from the Price house.

Jean spoke up. "We may have another clue," she said, and showed the officer the warning note. "This came in one of the snowballs."

As Officer Hodge gazed at the message, Jean suddenly noticed that there were faint scratches on the paper. Had they been made by the same ring which had marred the sheet received by Professor Crandall? Since the professor had requested that his note not be made public, Jean said nothing about the marks.

Presently Officer Hamer returned, and after doing some further investigating of the area, the two men drove off. Jean then told Louise of her observation.

"*Hmm*—so the ring wearer is trying to frighten us off the case," said Louise.

The Danas spent a few more minutes looking for further clues to the snowball thrower. They could find nothing but a jumble of snowy footprints, most of which were their own and those of the officers.

"We'd better start back to Starhurst," said Louise.

The two girls decided to go home by way of the street. They took a slightly circuitous route in order to pause at the frozen fountain.

"Louise," Jean said suddenly, "do you realize the basin is filled to the top with ice? When we saw it the other day it was only half full."

"You're right," Louise agreed. "And it hasn't rained or snowed since that time."

Jean suggested that someone had turned on the water. But who? And why had he done it? And how? The Danas were sure that the water in the old homestead must have been turned off long ago.

"Another mystery for us to solve!" said Jean with a chuckle as the girls left the fountain and cut across the property to the sidewalk.

Just before reaching it, they heard a loud crash. "Sounded like a car collision down the street!" Louise exclaimed. She and Jean broke into a run.

A moment later the Danas could see that the accident had occurred at the next corner.

"Jean!" cried Louise. "It's a delivery truck and —and *the station wagon from Starhurst School!* I can see the name on the side!"

There was a lone driver in the station wagon. He sat rigidly behind the wheel, apparently stunned.

Louise caught her breath sharply. "Oh, who is it?"

CHAPTER V

Police Tip

As LOUISE and Jean reached the scene of the accident, they were greatly alarmed to see that the person in the station wagon was Professor Crandall! The driver of the truck was standing alongside him, waving a fist in the professor's face and yelling:

"You crazy old man! Why don't you watch where you're going?"

The professor sat rigid and mute. But the instant the Dana girls appeared, he snapped out of his trancelike state and said to them, "The accident wasn't my fault."

Louise opened the door of the station wagon and asked, "Are you all right, Professor Crandall?"

"I—I guess so. Just shaken up."

The driver of the meat-market truck, a bristle-haired blond youth, continued to rant. "This old geezer ought to lose his license! He can't tell red from green!"

The professor, regaining his composure, looked the driver straight in the eye. "*You* ran into *me*, trying to beat the light."

"That's right," said an indignant voice. The speaker was one of two women who had just rushed up to the group of onlookers.

The speaker went on, "I'm Mrs. Treat. My friend here and I saw the whole accident from my house. The light had turned and the station wagon started across on the green light. This young man was driving down the other street so fast he couldn't stop and rammed right into the Starhurst car."

"I'll testify to that," said the other woman.

The truck driver, who said his name was Herby Sommers, lost his bluster. He admitted he was travelling at a good clip. "I jammed on my brakes, but skidded onto the intersection and hit the station wagon."

Jean demanded, "Why didn't you tell the truth in the first place?"

Herby did not reply, for at that moment a police car arrived. Mrs. Treat said she had phoned for it.

While one officer took pictures of the accident scene, the other wrote down the facts and gave the professor and Herby summonses to appear in court.

As soon as it was determined that the professor was actually unharmed, and the two vehicles could proceed under their own power, the police got ready to leave. First, however, they took down the names of the two women witnesses and of the Dana girls.

Suddenly the officers looked intently at the sisters, and one said, "Aren't you girls the amateur detectives of Starhurst?"

The sisters smiled and admitted that they were. One of the officers introduced himself as McGuire, the other as Kane.

"You've done some fine sleuthing in Penfield and other places," Officer McGuire said. "Maybe you both would like to know that the police department has just received an anonymous tip. Several suspected criminals may be hiding in this area. They're reported to be on their way to Chicago. Perhaps you'll spot them."

Louise and Jean were interested at once, and Jean asked, "What are their names?"

"Unfortunately we don't know," Officer McGuire replied. "No names were given."

Mrs. Treat turned to Herby and asked, "Who was the man that jumped from your truck at the time of the collision?"

"I don't know," Herby answered nervously. "You—you think he might be one of those crooks?"

"Why not?" Mrs. Treat said.

Officer McGuire turned to the delivery driver and demanded, "Why didn't you mention your passenger?"

Herby hung his head. "He was a hitchhiker. My boss doesn't allow me to give rides. That's why I didn't say anything."

"Your boss is right," Officer McGuire said sternly. "It's dangerous to pick up hitchhikers. What induced you to break the rule?"

Herby looked more uncomfortable than ever. He was already in great trouble and did not wish to add more! After a few moments' thought he said, "I suppose I may as well come clean. The guy offered me five dollars if I'd bring him out this way. I figured my boss wouldn't find out and I really could use the money."

"This may be more serious than you think, Herby," said Officer Kane. "What did your passenger look like?"

"Well, he was of medium height. Had red hair —real red hair—and I think blue eyes. Nothing special about his voice. He didn't talk much. That's all I can remember about him."

The officer said the information might be valuable; at least he would pass it along to his superiors. He and McGuire got into their car and drove off. Herby climbed behind the wheel of his truck, backed around, and slowly headed toward town.

Louise offered to drive the station wagon back to school and Professor Crandall readily assented. "My plan was certainly disrupted," he said wryly. "I was on my way to meet you girls and take a look at the fountain. Is it still all right?"

"Yes," Jean answered, "although we were surprised to see the basin filled with ice. The other day it was only half full. Also, there's no snow on top of it now."

The professor frowned. "Oh, I hope no one is tampering with the fountain!"

The girls urged him to remove the Cellini masterpiece as soon as possible, but he shook his head, saying that the transferal would have to wait for spring.

As soon as the Danas reached the dormitory, Louise went to the phone and called Mr. Black, the agent. She discussed the incident of the fountain with him, and he frankly admitted he was puzzled.

"The water in the homestead which supplied the fountain was turned off months ago," he said. "It looks as if someone deliberately poured water into the basin to fill it. But why?"

Louise said that she and Jean too were puzzled. After she had hung up, Louise wondered if perchance boiling water had been poured into the basin to melt the snow and ice. But again, what was the purpose?

The Danas barely had a chance for a quick breakfast before their first class. Although they tried to keep their minds on the work, and did obtain good grades for the day, their thoughts kept shifting to the mystery. Late that afternoon Jean told her sister she could not wait another minute for

the police report on the Price homestead and was
going to call headquarters.

She was given some interesting and startling
information by Captain James. The police believed
the footprints which Louise had uncovered belonged to a man named Thomas "Red" Shanley.
His fingerprints had been found in the house and
identified.

"Shanley is wanted as a forger," said Captain
James. "This definitely puts him in our area, and
we believe he is a member of the same gang we got
the tip about."

Jean exclaimed, "Then he could be the person
who stole the art objects from the house! And,
Captain, do you think he is the man who was riding
with Herby Sommers?"

"I'll know in a few minutes," the officer answered. "We sent for Herby. He has just walked
in. Hold the line while I see if he can identify the
picture we have of Red Shanley."

Presently the captain came back on the phone and
told Jean that Herby's red-haired passenger was
indeed the wanted forger.

"No wonder he disappeared in such a hurry!"
Jean remarked. "But one thing baffles me, Captain.
Why would he take refuge in an ice-cold house?
Did he steal the valuable art objects?"

"That's very possible," Captain James replied.
"Miss Dana, I advise you and your sister to proceed

very carefully in your detective work. Red Shanley is dangerous."

Jean promised that they would be cautious, then said good-by. She hurried off to tell Louise the latest developments in the case. Evelyn and Doris, now feeling fine, were also in the Dana suite.

When Jean had finished, Louise remarked, "We're beginning to gather some evidence, but we're a long way from finding out who sent Professor Crandall and us the warning notes."

Doris and Evelyn were disturbed by the turn of events.

That evening Louise and Jean were called to the school office. Professor and Mrs. Crandall were there with a couple whom the headmistress introduced as Mr. and Mrs. John Murray. Both had black hair and piercing eyes. They were of average height and slender. Mrs. Murray wore a fur coat and her husband had on an expensive-looking tweed overcoat.

"We are the people who have bought the Price homestead," said Mrs. Murray to the Danas. "We learned that Professor Crandall has purchased the fountain, but we will not think of letting it go."

"Indeed not," said Mr. Murray. "We have offered the professor not only the price he paid for the fountain, but a generous profit besides."

Mrs. Murray's face stiffened. "The professor does not seem inclined to sell, but we insist upon it."

Professor Crandall rose from his chair with fire smouldering in his eyes. Louise and Jean saw that he was trying hard to control his anger.

"Insist!" he began. "You are not in the position to insist! I won't sell and I won't be intimidated." He paused and looked sternly at the Murrays. "And furthermore, I will not tolerate threatening notes!"

CHAPTER VI

Quick Thinking

THE Danas were startled at Professor Crandall's words. Mr. and Mrs. Murray arose quickly and faced the elderly man. Their faces were red and their eyes fiery.

"We didn't come here to be insulted!" Mrs. Murray exclaimed angrily. "I don't know what threatening notes you're talking about."

"Professor Crandall," Mr. Murray said coldly, "that's a very harsh accusation. Evidently you're in some kind of trouble, but we had nothing to do with it. You'd better watch your tongue!"

Professor Crandall seemed in no mood to retract his statement, so his wife said quickly, "I realize no one should be hasty in judging others. Please sit down and let's talk about this calmly."

Louise and Jean were relieved when the Murrays appeared to be mollified. "It is true," Mrs. Crandall told the couple, "that my husband has

been warned by some unknown person not to remove the fountain. He has Mr. Black's permission
to leave it there until spring, which will be a more
feasible time to move it."

The Murrays insisted that the garden at the Price
homestead would be ruined if the fountain were
taken away. Mrs. Murray said, somewhat sarcasti-
cally, "What is your special interest in this fountain,
Professor Crandall?"

"I do not think it necessary for me to answer that
question." The elderly man bristled. "I have told
you I do not wish to sell the Cellini fountain and
that decision is final."

Mr. Murray shrugged. "Have it your own way.
At least my wife and I can enjoy it until spring."

During the course of this conversation, Louise
and Jean had been discreetly signalling to each
other. Louise had pointed to her little finger and
Jean understood this to mean that Mr. Murray was
not wearing a ring on either hand. The sisters came
to the same conclusion: although it was possible he
might sometimes wear a ring, it did not seem likely
that Mr. Murray had been the writer of the warning
notes.

Mrs. Crandall now said, "Louise and Jean, I
called you in to meet Mr. and Mrs. Murray because
of your interest in their new home. I think they are
entitled to know that you heard someone in the
house who ran out the back way soon after you
went in."

Secretly Louise and Jean felt that perhaps it had been unwise for the headmistress to mention this to the Murrays. They figured the story of the intruder and the theft of valuable art objects from the house should come from Mr. Black.

The girls smiled, nevertheless, and told the couple of having been caught in the blizzard and how they had broken into the house to get out of the storm. "All we had to do was ignite the logs which someone had laid in the fireplace. We enjoyed its warmth until the snow let up," said Louise.

Jean added, "No fire ever felt so good! We're sorry we had to break a windowpane but we have already paid for a new one to be put in."

The Murrays seemed only mildly interested and for a second time they arose, saying they must leave. After they had gone, Professor Crandall burst out, "I don't like those people! I don't trust them!"

Jean's eyes crinkled in merriment. "I don't either, Professor Crandall. But we have absolutely no evidence against them."

Louise explained their theory about the fact that Mr. Murray wore no ring. The professor finally conceded that one should not jump to a conclusion.

The subject of where the fountain might be placed on the school grounds was discussed for a few minutes. Mrs. Crandall reminded her husband that so far workmen had found no feasible spot over a natural spring.

"Both the professor and I," the headmistress told the Danas, "feel that it would be too costly to dig a long trench and run a pipe from the main building."

The Danas felt sorry for Professor Crandall. He rarely expressed a desire to have anything for himself. Now that the kindly man had found something that meant a great deal to him, it seemed too bad his dream could not be realized.

To cheer him up, Louise said, "I'm sure the problem can be solved when milder weather comes."

The professor gave her a warm smile of appreciation. "I hope you're right," he said.

Before returning to their suite, Louise and Jean decided to telephone Mr. Black and ask him if he had ever seen a ring on Mr. Murray's finger. Louise made the call. The agent said that he had not.

"I'm sure I would have noticed a ring," he said, "because making jewelry is a hobby of mine."

Resignedly the sisters went upstairs. Jean remarked, "Well, Louise, I guess that confirms our theory that Mr. Murray did not write the warning notes."

Louise nodded agreement.

The following day Mr. Norton, the assistant instructor in athletics, announced that all students who wanted to participate in the skating competition and exhibition should attend the practice session that afternoon at two-thirty. Louise and Jean were on the pond promptly. There was general skating for a warm-up which lasted half an hour, then each girl began to work on her speciality.

As Louise danced gracefully on the ice to the rhythm of music from a tape recorder, Lettie Briggs watched her enviously from the shore. Lettie was an awkward skater, and although there was no rule against her taking part in the competition, she knew she would have no chance against the more proficient contestants.

"Louise Dana makes me sick," Doris overheard Lettie say to Ina. "She thinks of herself as a big star and hopes someday to be chosen for the Olympics!"

Ina merely nodded her head. Long ago she had learned that it did not pay to disagree with Lettie.

In a few minutes the ice was cleared to give the racers a chance to practise. This was to be a race not only against time, but against various obstacles. These were to be either skated around or jumped over. The girls suffered several spills as they bumped into one another or failed to hurdle a low fence set up on the ice.

It was evident from the start that Jean Dana was far more skilled than her classmates.

Again Lettie showed every sign of being consumed with envy. "I can't stand it!" she told Ina. "Those smug Danas! I'll be back in a while." She skirted the pond and disappeared into the woods.

A little later the ice was cleared once more.

Jean's friends began to call out, "Let's see how fast you can skate around the edge of the pond."

Laughingly Jean consented. When she reached the far side Jean built up tremendous speed and many of the students began to clap. As she was about to round a curve, a large object flew through the air and landed on the ice directly in front of her.

There was no time for Jean to skirt the four-foot long, hip-high object, nor could she stop. The onlookers gasped and many closed their eyes, expecting Jean to take a frightful header. Instead, she gave a mighty leap and landed safely on the other side of the obstacle.

"She made it! Thank goodness!" Louise exclaimed.

Evelyn looked grave. She whispered to Doris and Louise, "I'll just bet Lettie Briggs did that! Let's go after her."

Several other girls who stood nearby were equally angry with the person who had thrown an aluminium roadblock in Jean's path. It had been used during the time the school was being rebuilt after a bad fire. Apparently the block had been discarded in the woods.

Louise and her friends took off their skates and quickly changed into boots which had been left in a small tool house near the pond. By the time they were ready for their pursuit of Lettie, Jean had joined them. Many of the spectators praised her alertness and skill, and said they were glad she had not been injured.

When Jean heard of her friends' suspicion and their decision to trail Lettie, she quickly said she would join them. All the others but Louise started out. She waited until her sister had changed into boots.

The sisters skirted the pond, then Jean asked, "Which way were the girls going?"

"I guess they plan to follow Lettie's prints in the snow."

These proved to be some distance to the left from where Jean thought the roadblock had been thrown. "Maybe Lettie didn't throw it. Anyway, let's look in that other direction first."

As the two girls approached the spot they noticed a set of very large boot prints which headed toward the pond and then back among the trees.

"Louise!" Jean exclaimed. "These weren't made by Lettie! Someone else tried to injure me."

Her sister agreed. "That someone is a big man, according to the size of these prints."

"It looks as though we have another enemy!" Jean speculated. "And a mean one!"

Louise did not reply. She had leaned down to examine the prints more carefully and now pointed out that the boots had three raised parallel lines on the sole.

"This is excellent identification," she said in excitement. "Let's follow these prints!"

The sisters hurried along but had not gone far when they heard terrified screams.

"It's one of the girls!" Jean cried out.

The Danas started running in the direction from which the screams had come. They wondered if the person who had hurled the roadblock had tried another vicious trick!

CHAPTER VII

The Phantom Skater

In a moment the Dana girls caught up to their friends who were following Lettie's trail.

"Who screamed?" Louise asked them quickly.

"We don't know," Evelyn replied. "We were worried it was you!"

At that moment the girls heard another scream and all rushed toward the sound. In a few seconds they saw Lettie in the distance struggling with a large blond-haired woman. The stranger was wearing slacks, boots, a heavy jacket, and a visored cap pulled down over her long, untidy hair.

"Leave her alone!" Jean yelled.

The entire group began to shout and the woman ran off.

When the girls reached Lettie, she was leaning against a tree and trembling violently. She was on the verge of tears and babbled, "Th-that horrible woman! I hope I never see her again!"

"Why was she fighting with you?" Doris asked Lettie.

"B-because I saw her!" Lettie stammered. "She-she was the one who threw that thing at you, Jean. She tried to make me promise I wouldn't tell anybody."

"And when you wouldn't promise," Evelyn spoke up, "she struck you?"

"Yes," Lettie replied. "She said if I ever told, I'd get worse punishment. She-she's a maniac!"

Louise spoke up kindly, "You can stop worrying, and we'll pretend you never said a word. My sister and I already have a clue to the identity of the person who tried to injure Jean."

Lettie looked relieved. "How?" she asked.

For answer Jean pointed to the ground. The telltale boot prints with the three parallel bars were plainly visible. To herself she was thinking, "Of course we didn't know the person was a woman. Lettie really gave us an added clue."

"What did this woman look like?" Jean asked Lettie.

"She had kind of large features and heavy eyebrows. Her voice was sort of deep—and boy, was she strong!"

Lettie started back toward the school and the other girls followed. Jean caught up to her and asked, "Why did you come into the woods?"

"That's my business," Lettie answered flippantly. She did not even thank the others for rescuing her. Instead, she remarked tartly, "Mrs. Crandall should give Starhurst students more protection."

Jean, disgusted at Lettie's attitude, decided to tease her and said impishly, "These woods are off limits to people who don't get permission to enter them."

Lettie gave Jean a sideways look, not knowing whether to believe her or not. She had never heard of such a rule—and neither had Jean—but Lettie felt that possibly she had neglected to read it in the school regulations.

The whole episode disturbed Mrs. Crandall very much. She at once notified police headquarters, and two men were sent to talk to Lettie and the Danas. The sisters gave as complete an account as possible.

Lettie added nothing to her story, except to say, "I know someone on the other side of the woods who sells maple syrup and candy. I was going there to order some for my parents."

The officers had never seen nor heard of a blond woman fitting the description given them, but said they would be on the lookout for her.

During the period between the end of the evening study hour and the lights-out bell, Evelyn came to the Danas' room. She reported having overheard part of a conversation Lettie was having with someone on the telephone.

"She called him Charlie and was just finishing a report on what had happened to her today. She added, 'I'll figure out some other way to pick up the stuff.' "

Jean asked, "Did she say what the 'stuff' was?"

Evelyn shook her head. "Maybe that maple syrup and candy she told the police about."

Jean giggled. "I bet Lettie has a boy friend we haven't met!"

The other two girls laughed. Lettie occasionally had a date, but usually he was someone she had invited—the supercilious girl rarely was asked out by boys. Louise suggested that maybe Charlie was Lettie's escort for the day of the skating competition.

With all the exercise and excitement the Danas had had that day, they fell asleep as soon as they got into bed. Around midnight Louise awakened. For a moment she thought it was morning because the room seemed so bright. Then she realized that the full moon was shining directly in her face.

By now she was wide awake and began to feel thirsty. "Guess I'll get a drink of water," she said to herself.

Louise slipped on her robe and slippers and walked down the corridor toward the rear of the building. She glanced out a window at the attractive snowy landscape bathed in bright moonlight. How beautiful it was! she thought.

As Louise's eyes roved over the scene, they came to rest on the school pond. Her attention was suddenly arrested by a lone skater dressed in a white suit, gliding effortlessly in a circle. Was the figure a man or a woman?

"That person is almost ghostlike!" Louise reflected. "Surely it's not a student. Maybe a member of the faculty or someone from town?"

The illusion of a phantom skater was so perfect that had a second white-suited skater not appeared from the woods, Louise might have convinced herself she was seeing something supernatural. The two figures began skating together, doing such intricate footwork, waltz jumps, spins, and axels that Louise was fascinated.

"They're as good as professionals," she murmured. "Oh, if I could only skate like that!"

Within ten minutes the couple climbed the slope at the pond's far edge and disappeared into the woods. Still very curious about the identity of the skaters, Louise got her drink of water and returned to bed.

She awakened early the next morning. Inspired by the flawless performance she had seen at midnight, Louise determined to go out to the pond immediately and practise her own dance on skates. To her satisfaction, she went through the routine perfectly.

"I hope I can do as well in the competition," Louise thought hopefully. She had time before breakfast to practise a combination of jumps she had trouble with sometimes.

As Louise neared the spot where the phantom skaters had entered the woods, she noticed a white scarf lying on the embankment. She swerved, and skated over to pick it up. The knitted scarf definitely belonged to a woman, and was expensive. In one corner was a tiny store label. It said: *Walpole's, New York City.*

"Not much clue to the owner," Louise thought. Instinctively she peered underneath the label, which was sewn on only at the ends. Printed in ink on the back of it were the initials B. C.

Louise decided to take the scarf to the dormitory. Her sister was fascinated to hear of the midnight skaters but baffled as to their identity. Neither of the girls could think of anyone at school with the initials B. C.

"I'll ask Mrs. Crandall," Louise offered.

A little later she met the headmistress at the door to the dining room and handed her the white scarf, explaining where she had found it.

"No one at Starhurst has those initials," Mrs. Crandall said. "But I will show the scarf during breakfast. Perhaps someone here will recognize it."

There was no claimant, however, so Louise felt sure that it belonged to one of the phantom skaters. When Louise finished her class assignments that afternoon, she walked over to the pond.

A detective from the Penfield police force was

there. He introduced himself as Sam Gibbons and explained he had been assigned to the school because of the blond woman's attack on Lettie Briggs.

Louise asked if anyone had inquired about a lost scarf. The guard shook his head.

Then Louise asked if there was any news of Red Shanley, the forger. Gibbons said No, but that the police were still on the lookout for him.

"How about that large blond woman? Any trace of her?" Louise queried.

"Not yet, but our men have been alerted."

A few minutes later Jean joined her sister and said, "Let's go over to the homestead and look around."

Louise introduced Detective Gibbons who said, "I think it'll be all right. But don't you girls go *into* the house by yourselves."

"We've already promised Mrs. Crandall we wouldn't," said Jean.

Detective Gibbons smiled. "One of our police cars will be cruising past the Price place at intervals. If there's any trouble, signal for help."

The sisters entered the woods and headed straight for their destination. As they neared the garden, they were surprised to hear chopping sounds.

"I wonder what's going on?" Jean said.

The Danas started to run. Suddenly Jean grasped Louise's arm. "Listen!" she said. The girls stopped.

There was not a sound. The chopping had ceased.

The Danas pushed on. As they reached the Cellini fountain, the sisters stared in astonishment. Someone had been hacking at the ice on the nymph figures and in the basin!

"Now who did this?" Jean asked indignantly.

Louise was staring at the ground. "I can make a good guess. Look at those boot prints!"

Jean's eyes widened. "The big blond woman!"

CHAPTER VIII

Doubling Back

IMPRINTED in the snow, from the boot soles, were the three telltale parallel marks!

"The big blond woman!" Jean repeated in astonishment. "Was *she* chopping ice away from the fountain?"

Louise pointed out that there were many different footprints around the area. It would be hard to say whether the woman actually did the chopping. Nevertheless, the Danas concluded that the boot prints were more recent than any of the other marks.

"I have a hunch the husky blonde is guilty," Jean declared.

"But why would she want to chip off the ice?" Louise asked, puzzled.

"It's beyond me," Jean answered. "Let's follow the prints and see where they go."

The trail led directly to the homestead. Whether or not the woman had entered the house could not be ascertained. The snow on the steps and front porch had been so trampled by all the investigators that it was impossible even to make a guess.

Jean set her jaw. "If that woman is inside, I'm going to ask her why she threw the roadblock at me!"

With that, Jean marched up and pounded on the door. Silence. Again she rapped loudly. No one appeared. After a third knock without a response, Louise said, "The mysterious woman might be in the house, all right. But I doubt she'd come to the door."

"Especially if she's mixed up in some crooked scheme," Jean had to agree. "Maybe we can find a clue if we walk around the house."

The sisters made their way across the front of the building and turned down one side. They looked at the ground for dropped articles, new and different footprints, or anything else unusual.

They were so intent on their work they were unaware that a huge mass of snow had become loosened from the steeply gabled roof. The next moment the snow thundered downward like an avalanche, knocking the girls over and covering them completely.

Jean, though stunned, managed to extricate herself from the fluffy white mass and took a long, deep breath. Suddenly she realized that Louise, who had been some distance from her, was not in sight.

"She must be buried!" Frantically Jean dug down through the snow where she had last seen her sister standing. She could not find Louise and panic seized her. Louise might be smothered before she could be rescued!

"I must keep cool!" Jean thought.

She looked around. One section of the heavy snow seemed deeper than the rest. Hopefully Jean dug into this area and finally touched the back of her sister's sport coat. Tugging hard, she managed to free Louise. Her eyes were closed and she sagged limply as Jean pulled her to a sitting position. But Louise was still breathing and in a few seconds the fresh air revived her entirely.

"Boy, you certainly gave me a scare!" said Jean.

"I don't think that avalanche happened of its own accord," Louise said weakly.

"You mean—someone started it?" Jean asked in surprise.

"Yes, I do." Louise explained that just before the snow had hit her, she had heard mocking laughter from above. Then a man's deep voice had said, "You were warned to stay away!"

Jean looked upward and saw an open window in one of the third-story dormers. "That means someone *is* in the house!" she said.

All this time the two girls had been brushing the

snow from their clothing. The Danas felt sure their every move was being followed.

"We'll pretend to leave," Jean whispered, "then backtrack and watch the house."

The sisters, staying a safe distance from the building, hurried to the front and down the walk. Louise pointed out the well-trampled snow. "Lots of people have been around," she observed, "including the police, probably."

When they reached the sidewalk, Louise and Jean walked for a short distance before re-entering the grounds. They looked for a cruising police car, but none appeared. Keeping behind a screen of trees, the sisters made their way to a spot from which they could watch both the front and rear doors of the homestead without being detected.

While waiting, each of the young sleuths was trying to figure out what had happened. The dormer window was still open. Had the person who caused the avalanche not taken time to close it and fled as hastily as possible?

"Or maybe he's still inside," said Jean. "I'll bet he tried to frighten us away so he can carry on some kind of work in the house that he doesn't want us to know about."

Louise and Jean had not taken their eyes from the house. Suddenly they saw the front door open. The next moment a man appeared, slammed the door, and turned to come down the porch steps.

Mr. Black!

The sisters exchanged amazed glances. Was the estate agent involved in the mystery?

"Let's go!" Jean urged, and ran toward the house. Louise followed.

As they emerged from the wooded area and confronted Mr. Black, the man stepped back, startled. "You frightened me," he said, irritated. "Why did you jump out at me like that? You playing some game?"

The Danas were embarrassed and apologized. Promptly, however, the sisters told him a straightforward story of what had happened, and asked if he had seen anyone in the house.

"No. I got here just a few minutes ago and didn't see or hear anything. That avalanche of snow must have happened just before I arrived."

The Danas were too polite to argue with him. A startling thought flashed through their minds: Was he the person who had caused the avalanche? They pointed out that a dormer window on the third floor was open. He turned and stared at it in such utter astonishment that the sisters were convinced he knew nothing about it.

The agent frowned and said, "I'll close it. It seems to me the police aren't doing a very good job of guarding this place!"

"That's right," Jean agreed. "As we came into the woods we heard chopping sounds and later discovered that someone has been chipping ice off the fountain."

Again Mr. Black frowned. "I'm sorry to hear that." Then he shrugged. "Of course the fountain is no longer my responsibility. It's the property of Professor Crandall. If he wants to leave it here until spring, that's his worry."

Louise and Jean thought the agent was certainly not being cooperative. Eager to get inside the house and look around, they followed Mr. Black as he returned and unlocked the front door. Although uninvited, the sisters followed him in.

"I'll go up and close that window," he said. "You'd better not come in case of any trouble."

The Danas winked at each other, and as soon as Mr. Black disappeared up the stairway, they started a little sleuthing of their own. Jean rushed to the rooms at the rear, but found no one. The door to the cellar was bolted so she assumed no one was hiding there. Quickly Jean ascended the back stairway to the second floor.

Meanwhile, Louise had looked in the various front rooms of the house and now she ran up the main stairs. Together, the girls examined every second-floor room, but came upon no one, and nothing to indicate anyone had been there.

As they finished their search and met in the centre of the hall, Mr. Black was just descending the stairs from the third floor. He looked at the girls questioningly. Louise said quickly, "We didn't see anybody downstairs so we thought we would check here. Did you find anything suspicious upstairs?"

"Not a thing. It certainly is a mystery how that window got open."

"Mr. Black, do you mind if Louise and I take a look up there?" Jean asked.

The realtor thought for a moment. The Danas guessed what was probably going through his mind: Did these young sleuths think they could find something he had missed? Rather grudgingly he said, "All right. Go ahead. But don't be long. I have to get back."

Louise and Jean ran up the steps and went directly to the room where the dormer window had been open. Along one wall lay a stout stick about six feet in length.

On a hunch Jean knelt down to feel the stick. "It's wet!" she cried out. "This is what that awful man used to push the snow on top of us!"

"If so," said Louise, "that big blond woman was here with him."

"How do you figure that?" her sister asked.

Jean turned and looked at Louise who was staring at the floor. Near the window, imprinted in the soft, well-worn pine wood, were two distinct boot prints. On the sole of each were the three parallel lines!

From the floor below Mr. Black called up, "Did you girls find a clue?"

"Yes," Louise told him. "Please come up."

When the agent appeared, the sisters showed

him their discovery. Mr. Black stared in astonished disbelief.

Louise told him of their suspicions that a large blond woman was connected with the mystery and that she had left her telltale boot prints in a number of other places.

Jean asked, "Mr. Black, do *you* know a big, tall, blond woman?"

The Danas thought the agent gave a slight start at the question, and eagerly awaited his answer.

CHAPTER IX

The Gorilla-Man

Mr. Black did not reply immediately. He looked quizzically at the Danas.

Finally he said, "No."

"Do you think the blond woman may be a friend of Mr. and Mrs. Murray?" Jean asked.

"I have no idea," the agent answered. In a friendlier tone he added, "By the way, Mrs. Murray came to my office this morning. She is trying to persuade me to let her keep the fountain at the homestead. I don't know why the woman has her heart set on it, but she has offered to pay Professor Crandall even more than the sum she first mentioned to him."

The Danas were surprised at Mrs. Murray's persistence and said so. Jean added, "I'm sure Professor Crandall won't part with the Cellini fountain under any circumstances. He wants it for the Starhurst grounds."

Louise expressed alarm over the hacking of the

ice on the fountain. "Someone may be trying to deface it."

Mr. Black looked puzzled. "Why should a person want to do that? Spoiling its beauty isn't going to help anybody."

With a sigh Louise admitted she could not figure it out, either. "Jean and I also can't understand why there's so much mysterious activity in connection with the fountain."

Mr. Black smiled. "I'm surprised that you girl detectives haven't solved that mystery long before this." There was a note of sarcasm in his voice. "Well, I must be on my way. Can I give you a lift back to school?"

"No, thank you," said Louise. "We'd rather walk."

The girls decided to return to school by way of the woods. They said good-bye to the agent and walked down the path leading to the garden. As they stopped to gaze once more at the ice-covered fountain glittering in the sunlight, Jean remarked, "I'm dying to see what this looks like unfrozen."

"Those dancing nymphs must be beautiful, and with water flowing over them, really picturesque," Louise commented.

"I hope," said Jean, "that Professor Crandall takes our advice and moves the fountain right away. But the poor man is so absent-minded that he'll probably forget all about it."

"Then we'll just have to keep after him," Louise declared. As the girls walked toward Starhurst, she added, "Maybe we're making too much out of this mystery. Mischievous boys from town could be responsible for the ice-chopping."

"I doubt that," Jean replied. "This is too far out of Penfield and not close enough to the road to be a likely target for pranksters."

The sisters trudged on and presently saw Doris and Evelyn making their way toward them. When the girls met, Evelyn asked, "Any more excitement?"

The Danas took turns telling about the avalanche, the open window, the boot prints with three parallel bars, the chopping of the ice on the fountain, and their meeting with Mr. Black.

Doris giggled. "Profitable afternoon."

"Yes," Louise said, "but still no solutions."

Jean declared that someday soon she was going to find the big blond woman. "Nobody can throw things at me and get away with it!" she said angrily. "I want to ask her a few questions!"

"I don't blame you for being mad," said Evelyn.

Louise told her Mr. Black was going to make a report to headquarters on the latest findings. "I hope they'll pick her up soon so we can talk to her."

"It's my guess," said Doris, "that if the woman thinks she's a suspect, she'll—"

Doris stopped speaking. Her eyes suddenly bulged, and she gave a wild shriek.

"What's the matter?" Evelyn asked quickly.

Doris seemed paralyzed with fright. Unable to speak, she merely pointed. The other girls whirled and looked toward the trees a few yards distant. What they saw made them all gasp in horror.

"It's—it's an abominable snowman!" Evelyn cried out.

A huge white shaggy gorilla was stalking menacingly toward the girls!

The creature was swinging its arms and now began to utter frightening growls.

"Run!" Evelyn urged.

The four girls took to their heels, sprinting at top speed back toward the homestead. When they were safely beyond reach of the shaggy white monster, they all stopped to catch their breath.

The quartet looked back, and were relieved to see that their pursuer apparently had given up.

"What was it?" gasped Doris, still shaking.

"He probably escaped from a zoo," Evelyn answered in a quivering voice.

Jean said, "I never heard of a white gorilla!"

"Nor I," Louise agreed. "It's my opinion there's something phony about him. Let's try to find out."

"Not me," Doris said firmly. "I'm going back to school, by way of the street."

Evelyn hesitated, torn by curiosity and not wanting to desert her friends should the monster menace them again in the woods. Finally she decided to go with Doris.

"You Danas watch your step!" Evelyn warned. "I know you can run faster than he can, but just the same he might trap you somehow."

"Okay," said Jean. She and Louise started off in the other direction. They kept alert, but did not see or hear the strange creature. They did pick up his huge tracks, which turned from the spot where they had first seen him and went toward Starhurst School.

"If that gorilla ever puts in an appearance at school, he'll scare the girls out of their wits," Louise said, frowning.

"We must stop him!" Jean declared.

She started running, following his tracks. Louise was close behind, but kept looking left and right and to the rear.

Suddenly Jean called, "Louise! The gorilla's footprints stop here!"

Louise hurried over and the two girls stared at the ground. From the spot where the big prints ended, a series of smaller ones, belonging to a man wearing a medium-sized boot, continued.

"So someone was wearing a costume," said Louise.

"But why? And who is the gorilla-man?" Jean asked.

Both girls guessed that the purpose of the grotesque disguise was to scare them and their friends from entering the woods again.

"It could be Red Shanley," Jean guessed. "We know he was here before."

"Yes. But I have a completely different idea," said Louise. "Do you think Lettie Briggs could be playing another joke on us? She might have asked her friend Charlie to play gorilla."

Jean laughed. "If Lettie set out to scare us, she certainly accomplished her purpose. Let's see if we can get any clues back at the dorm."

That evening the Danas unobtrusively watched Lettie and Ina. But neither Louise nor Jean detected any giggling between the two girls and no indication that they were enjoying a joke at the expense of the Danas.

Louise told Doris and Evelyn of finding evidence the "gorilla" was actually a man in costume. She suggested that they say nothing about the shaggy white creature to anyone at school, in case the whole thing *were* merely a joke.

"Okay. How about talking to Professor Crandall, though, about moving the fountain?" said Doris.

"We'll see him," Louise promised.

Before doing this, she and Jean checked with police headquarters for any news about the fountain, Red Shanley, or the blond woman. The girls learned from Captain James that so far no clues had been picked up. The officer promised to continue investigating.

Jean giggled. "Maybe they'll run into the gorilla-man!"

The Danas went to call on the Crandalls. The professor became alarmed upon hearing that the beautiful fountain might be wrecked. He looked at his wife with questioning eyes.

"Do you think we should go to the extra expense of trying to move it in this weather?" he asked.

Mrs. Crandall avoided a direct answer. Instead, she mentioned the high cost of labour and the fact that no one had yet found a suitable place for the fountain. "But I shall leave the entire matter in your hands."

Inwardly the Danas groaned. The professor was absent-minded, and besides, he was working on an important speech he was going to deliver at a nearby college. The sisters were sure the matter of moving the fountain would be put off. But he did promise to look into the matter at once.

The following day was Friday and the Danas were caught in the mounting excitement over the skating competition and the visit of the Walton Academy boys.

"We'd better take our minds off the mystery long enough to concentrate on our skating," said Jean to Louise with a grin.

"Right."

That morning the postman arrived early.

"There's something in our box!" Jean exclaimed to Louise.

Quickly she unlocked it and together the sisters studied the envelope. The address was typed, and the first line read: *Louise and Jean Dana, Detectives.* The postmark was New York City.

"This must be a joke," said Louise.

She tore open the envelope. As the two girls read the message, they stared in amazement. Typed on a single sheet were the words:

> *What that is hidden,*
> *Is in plain sight?*
> *Walk to the welcome spot*
> *And gaze to your right.*
> B. C.

CHAPTER X

The Missing Riddle

"How strange!" said Louise, and read the riddle over a couple of times. "B. C. again!"

Jean turned the sheet over, then looked carefully at the envelope, inside and out. There was not the slightest clue to the sender nor the meaning of the riddle.

"Do you suppose the initials B. C. stand for the name of the sender?" she asked.

Louise shrugged in complete bewilderment. "The only thing I can deduce is that the person who lost the scarf at our pond went on to New York and sent this. But who *is* B. C.?"

Doris and Evelyn came along then and were shown the note. Both confessed to being completely at a loss for an explanation. Several other girls in the mail room crowded around the Danas, including Lettie Briggs.

"Another mystery?" she asked, glancing over Jean's shoulder at the contents of the note.

"It seems to be," Louise answered. "But we'll try to solve it!"

Lettie raised her head and gave a supercilious grin. "Think you'll have any more luck than you've had in your—er—case at the Price homestead?"

Evelyn was indignant. "So you've been spying, eh? Maybe you think you could do better."

Lettie shrugged. "I'm sure I could, but I'm not the least bit interested. I have other, more important matters to attend to." She walked off loftily.

The Danas, feeling amused rather than annoyed, went up to their suite, still puzzling over the riddle.

"I have a strong hunch," said Louise, "that this riddle is definitely connected with the mystery we're trying to solve. We know the writer was probably here at Starhurst. The question is, did the woman I saw skating on the pond drop the scarf and also write this riddle?"

"And if so," Jean added, "why is she being so elusive?"

There was no further time for speculation. The girls gathered up books and homework and went off to their classes. Jean, looking out the window a little later, remarked that it had started to snow again.

"Oh, dear, I hope it won't spoil the ice for skating! Louise, do you realize Ken and Chris and

the other Walton boys will be here by dinnertime?"

Her sister grinned. "I can't wait!"

When Jean returned to the Danas' room just
before luncheon, she found Louise searching her
desk diligently. "Lose something, Sis?"

"Did you see me put down the riddle this morning?" Louise asked.

"Yes, right on top of your desk."

"I thought so too," Louise said, "but when I
came back, it was missing."

The sisters looked at each other in dismay. Both
had planned to study the riddle thoroughly as soon
as they had a chance. The words, however, were
firmly in their minds.

Louise speculated, "If it really has something to
do with the mystery—perhaps it's a clue—maybe
somebody didn't want the information left
around."

"Either that," Jean remarked, "or else Lettie
took it. She saw the paper, remember? I'm going to
ask Mrs. Crandall to let me announce at luncheon
that if anyone has it, please to return the riddle to
us."

Jean put her question to those in the dining
room, but received no response. After the meal she
went to the kitchen and spoke to the various maids
having their lunch, but all declared they had never
seen the riddle.

Later Evelyn came to the Danas and said she at

any rate was sure Lettie was playing another one of her tricks. "I'm going to find out!" she declared.

The Danas smiled in appreciation and Louise said, "Good luck!"

The snow continued for some time after classes were over, so there was no chance to skate. Louise was disappointed because she had hoped to perfect her double flip, a tricky manoeuvre which none of the other Starhurst contestants had tried.

Excited chatter in the dormitory grew louder as the girls prepared to greet their Walton Academy visitors. The boys would check into a small motel in Penfield and arrive at Starhurst in time for dinner.

There was a last-minute rush to set hair, sew on missing buttons, and press clothes. A wail from Doris could be heard far down the hall. The zipper on her lovely powder-blue dress had separated from the cloth!

"Oh, no! I can't stand it!" she cried. "Somebody help me, quick!"

Louise rushed down the hallway and other girls crowded into Doris's room. Louise scooped the dress up. "I'll take this back to my room and fix it."

"But it will take ages!" Doris said frantically. "The boys will be here in half an hour!"

Louise put her free arm around the distraught girl. "Please relax and powder your nose, and don't worry about a thing!"

"Oh, you're a darling!" Doris exclaimed. "I know you're a wonder at sewing. But how about yourself? You're not dressed yet."

"Just keep calm," Louise said soothingly. "I'm sure both of us will be downstairs on time."

Her prophecy turned out to be true. After the large group of boys had assembled in the spacious living room, all the girls came down to find their respective partners.

Louise was wearing a slim-fitting yellow princess dress, a lovely contrast to her dark hair. Jean's pale-green dress, a tailored two-piece, was enhanced by her pink cheeks. Both girls wore gold necklaces and bracelets.

Louise spotted a tall, handsome blond youth and hurried to greet him. "Ken!" she cried. "How wonderful to see you!"

"It seems like ages," he replied with an admiring look. "This week end is going to be neat."

In the meantime, Jean had found Chris and they were engaged in animated conversation. "Did you bring your best skating feet?" she teased.

Chris, dark-haired and full of fun, grinned. "I sure did," he answered. "What are the chances of you and me winning a prize together?"

Jean smiled. "Pretty good. We'll have a lot of competition, though, especially from that whiz hockey player of yours."

A few minutes later the dinner gong sounded

and the couples followed Professor and Mrs. Crandall into the dining room.

How changed the room was! Now there were tables for four, with attractive red tablecloths and napkins. In the centre of each was a candle and a vase of evergreens and red carnations in anticipation of the Christmas season. The Danas and their dates sat down at one of the tables.

"I'm glad we four are alone," said Chris. "Ken and I are dying to hear about your latest mystery."

Louise and Jean looked amazed. They had said nothing to the boys about their case for Professor Crandall. Seeing the girls' puzzled expressions, Ken laughed. "We don't know what the mystery is, but you girls never go long without one to solve."

Jean grinned. "You had us fooled for a moment," she said. "We thought you were mind readers!"

During the meal Louise and Jean told the boys about the frozen fountain and the strange happenings at the old Price homestead. Louise asked, "Would you like to go there and look around?"

"Would we!" Ken replied. "You mean tonight?"

Louise shook her head. "Tonight there's a dance here."

"I wouldn't miss that for anything," Chris said. "But how about our going over to the place tomorrow?"

Louise said that they hoped the pond would be

cleared of snow by morning so the two couples could practise for the afternoon's competition. "Later we can hike through the woods to the Price place."

"We'll be here at nine o'clock," said Ken. "Meet you on the ice."

At nine-fifteen the following morning there were many skaters on the pond. The ice was in excellent condition. First the figure skaters were given time for a workout. Bystanders thought that the footwork used by Louise and Ken was superb. The pair executed an overhead lift and received loud applause.

Jean and Chris found the competition very keen among their group. In the straight skating for pairs, their time was many seconds behind a girl named Marie Basler and her partner Tommy Pitt. These two also went over every obstacle without nicking one.

Jean and Chris increased their efforts, and did very well. After another half hour of practice, the two Danas and their dates changed into hiking clothes and started off into the woods through the fresh layer of snow.

Presently Louise remarked, "Not a footprint in sight. Boys, you should have seen this place yesterday. There were all sizes, including the huge gorilla-man's barefoot prints."

"I'd like to meet that monster," said Chris.

Jean chuckled. "You're a brave soul."

Finally the foursome came within view of the old homestead. Jean blinked, then cried out, "Smoke is coming from the roof! The house is on fire!"

The friends began to run. Suddenly Ken burst out laughing. "That's not smoke!" he said. "The sun is causing steam evaporation on the wet roof!"

Jean made a chagrined face. "Put me at the foot of the science class," she said.

The young people slowed to a walk and in a few seconds approached the frozen fountain. The boys stared at it intently and Chris remarked, "So this is the centre of the mystery!"

As Ken surveyed the bronze piece, his eyes narrowed. "It is a beauty, but the fountain would look better if it weren't tilted."

Louise and Jean looked at the piece more closely. "You're right!" said Louise. "The dancing nymphs and the rest of the fountain are definitely at an angle! They weren't before!"

Ken thought that perhaps frost had caused the ground to heave and thus disturb the fountain. But Jean remarked it had not been this way on the previous visit.

"I have an idea somebody has tampered with the fountain," she said. "It was done before the snow began to fall yesterday, because there's not a mark around here."

Louise was excited. "Let's dig around the base."

The four young people leaned down and with

their hands scooped up snow and tossed it aside.
They could see that the concrete foundation had
been chipped away and wooden wedges driven
under one side of the fountain's base.

"Somebody intends to take this fountain away!"
Chris exclaimed.

Before any of his companions had a chance to
respond, a man's deep voice yelled from nearby:

"Get out!"

Louise turned just in time to see a sandbag sail
toward them. Ken was directly in its path!

"Ken, watch out!" Louise called.

She was too late. The heavy bag hit Ken squarely
on one shoulder, knocking him over. He went
down with a thud.

CHAPTER XI

Close Competition

"KEN, you're hurt!" cried Louise. She leaned down to ascertain the extent of his injuries. Finding they were not serious, the three helped Ken to his feet.

Then Jean and Chris turned in the direction from which the sandbag had been thrown. Whoever had tossed it now had a head start in escaping!

"Suppose you look in that direction for footprints, Chris, and I'll watch for them over here," Jean said.

They had hardly separated before Chris called out, "I've picked some up."

Jean ran to his side and stared unbelievingly. Before her were large prints of boots which contained three parallel bars on the soles. Quickly she explained this clue to her companion.

"A woman!" he repeated. "She's really hefty!"

"And likes to throw things," said Jean, recalling the roadblock. "I wonder what happened to the man, though."

Jean and Chris started to follow the prints. They led toward the homestead through a heavily shrubbed area nearby, down the front walk, and into the street. Here they were lost in a mass of indistinguishable tire tracks.

Jean was disappointed. "We've been so near that woman several times but can't catch her!" she wailed.

Chris smiled. "Don't give up hope!"

The chase was abandoned and the couple returned to Louise and Ken. The blond youth declared that he was all right. "Never felt better in my life!" he said, thumping his chest.

Despite Ken's lightheartedness, the others were worried about his taking part in the competition that afternoon. Louise said perhaps they should give up the whole idea.

"Not a chance!" Ken exclaimed. "Believe me, Lou, I'm perfectly okay!"

"But what about your holding me up in the cartwheel lift?" Louise asked. "We'll have to leave that out."

"Nothing of the sort," Ken insisted. "If necessary, I'll get good old Doc Chris here to massage my shoulder. That'll loosen up the muscles—that is, if they decide to act balky."

He could not be dissuaded from entering the figure-skating competition with Louise, so that subject was dropped. The foursome had just decided to return to school, when they saw a policeman coming in their direction. He was Officer Kane. Louise introduced Ken and Chris. She described the sandbag attack, then informed him that someone had been tampering with the fountain.

"We're afraid someone may be trying to steal it," she said.

Kane scowled. "This is bad news," he said. "We haven't enough men to keep watch here around the clock. You'd better tell your professor to get busy and have the fountain moved."

"We already have." Jean sighed. "We'll remind him again."

Louise asked Officer Kane if there had been any clue to the tall blond woman. He shook his head. "Evidently she's very careful to keep out of sight."

The officer promised to relay the information about the sandbag incident to headquarters. "I'll examine the fountain base now," he said.

Jean glanced at her wristwatch. "I wish we could stay, but we'd better get back to school."

The young people made the trek through the woods without incident. As they reached the top of the slope above the pond, all of them exclaimed at the decorations which had been put up in their absence.

Varicolored bunting flew from atop poles set

back a distance from the ice. At one end of the pond stood a table and chairs for the judges. The table contained attractive prizes. Draped over a clotheshorse were the velvet capes and golden paper crowns for the queen and her escort.

Ken smiled at Louise. "You'd look lovely in the queen's cape and crown," he said.

Louise giggled. "I can't wear them unless you win the escort's costume."

Luncheon was served within a few minutes, then the boys returned to their motel to get ready for the competition. Louise seized the opportunity to tell Professor Crandall what had happened to the fountain.

A worried frown crossed his forehead. "Ah yes," he said, "I must do something about it. I'll call a trucking company at once."

"But, Professor Crandall," said Louise, "the fountain must be loosened from its foundation first. A stone mason will have to do that."

"True, true," the elderly man said. "Let me see. A man who once did some work here—his name is—oh yes, Alfred Hunt. I'll call him at once. Since I am forgetful, you'd better stand right alongside me and offer any helpful suggestions."

Louise looked up the mason's telephone number and dialled it. Then she handed over the instrument.

Mr. Hunt himself answered the phone and Professor Crandall told him what he wanted. Louise, who could distinctly hear Mr. Hunt's voice, was startled by his answer. "I have already been engaged by a Mr. Stevenson to loosen the fountain from its foundation."

"But he has no right to do that!" Professor Crandall protested. "I've bought the fountain."

"*You?*" the mason exclaimed. "Why, Mr. Stevenson claims he purchased it."

"That's not true," the professor insisted.

Louise whispered to him, "Get Mr. Stevenson's address."

Professor Crandall asked Mr. Hunt for it, but the mason refused. "I'm not going to be involved in any shady doings," he said. "I'd rather not have the job." With that, he hung up.

Professor Crandall was upset over this startling development. While he was thinking about his next move, Louise dialled police headquarters and reported the latest information to Captain James. "Try to find out who this Mr. Stevenson is, please, and let Professor Crandall know." The captain promised to do what he could.

Louise turned to the elderly man and urged him to call another stone mason immediately. He nodded, consulted the classified section of the telephone directory, and selected a mason named Mareno. The man proved to be very pleasant and cooperative. He said he would come to the school at once and get his instructions.

A short time later he arrived at the Starhurst

office. After hearing his assignment, Mr. Mareno said, "Professor Crandall, don't worry about anything. I'll take care not only of loosening the fountain, but I'll have a trucker friend bring it here." The kind-looking man added, "We'll deliver the fountain to you Monday evening without fail."

Professor Crandall thanked him profusely, and the Danas beamed. The mason said good-bye to them and left.

Louise and Jean hurried off to change into their special skating costumes. Louise's consisted of a white felt skirt embroidered in a red and green leaf design. She wore a snug-fitting sweater-blouse which was pure white except for the neck which was decorated with red and green sequins.

Jean put on a bright-red skirt and a long-sleeved sweater ornamented by tiny white snail shells.

The Danas met Ken and Chris at the pond where a three-piece band of high school boys was playing lively tunes. The scene was very gay and all the girl skaters looked most attractive. As usual, Lettie Briggs had chosen a very expensive costume—a pale-green velvet skirt and blouse trimmed with tiny rows of shirred white lace. Her escort, Jimmy Trask, who was shorter than she, wore heavy horn-rimmed glasses, and looked as if he would have preferred to be back at Walton Academy. Lettie kept up a continuous chatter to which he hardly listened.

Three judges, two women and a man, sat waiting

for the events to start. In a few moments Mrs.
Crandall stood up and spoke over a microphone
near the trophy table.

She welcomed all the guests, then turned the
microphone over to Mr. Norton, the assistant
athletic director. He announced that the first event
would be conventional skating by couples. They
would be judged entirely on form. The Danas were
not in this number. Evelyn Starr and her partner
won, with Doris Harland and her friend as runners-
up.

"Our next number," Mr. Norton announced,
"will be straight racing."

The Danas and their escorts had not entered this
contest but cheered the racers on. A student who
had come to Starhurst only the previous September
and her partner won. Everyone but Lettie ap-
plauded heartily. Her roommate, Ina, had been in
the race but had been eliminated early.

"Ina, you should have the prize," Lettie said in a
loud voice. "Besides, it isn't fair to give it to a new
girl!"

Her voice carried to the winner, who looked
very ill at ease. She quickly spoke to Mrs. Crandall,
saying perhaps Lettie was right, and that one of the
older girls should receive the award.

The headmistress looked annoyed at the suggestion. "The decision is the judges', not Miss
Briggs's!"

Everyone's attention was diverted from the incident when once more Mr. Norton spoke over the microphone. "Our next number will be an obstacle race. The skaters will gather speed around the edge of the pond and complete three full circles before going toward the middle where the obstacles will be set up." He asked that five small barrels be brought out and placed in a circle at the centre of the pond at twenty-foot intervals.

The rule for this event, the director went on, was that the partners were required to hold hands at all times, even while jumping the obstacles.

When the barrels were ready, Mr. Norton called out the names of the first contestants. They were Marie Basler and Tommy Pitt. The two put on a wonderful performance, and, so far as the onlookers could see, it was a perfect one. The applause was thunderous. The contestants were followed by three other couples, then Mr. Norton called out, "Our last contestants will be Jean Dana and Chris Barton!"

The straight racing was easy for the couple, and they developed terrific speed which won applause even before they turned toward the centre of the pond. Then, hand in hand and with Chris calling, "Now!" he and Jean sailed gracefully over the first barrel.

Straightening up from a crouch, they swung toward the second obstacle and went over it flawlessly. Encouraged now, they swerved and took the third, fourth, and fifth barrels smoothly.

"Yeah! Bravo!" came cries from the crowd.

Jean and Chris smiled and acknowledged the applause as they skated to the side to await the decision.

"Do we have a chance against Marie and Tommy?" Jean asked herself.

After a few minutes' conference, the three judges handed scoring sheets to Mr. Norton. He read them and approached the microphone. Everyone at the pond waited breathlessly for the announcement.

"It is the unanimous decision of the judges," he said, "that two couples shall share the honor of winning the obstacle race. Marie Basler and Tommy Pitt, and Jean Dana and Chris Barton!"

Amid wild applause and cheers, the four contestants shook hands with one another. Louise and Ken skated up. Louise gave her sister a big hug and said, "Just marvellous, honey!"

Jean squeezed her sister's arm and said, "I hope you have as much luck as I did."

When the excitement died down, Mr. Norton announced the last event on the programme. It would be figure skating in pairs. Lots had been drawn and Louise and Ken would perform last.

All the skaters ahead of them gave fine performances. Then Mr. Norton said, "And now our final contestants—Louise Dana and Ken Scott."

As Louise skated with her partner to the centre of the pond to await the start of the music, Jean began to worry. With Ken's bruised shoulder, would he be able to hold Louise in the cartwheel lift?

CHAPTER XII

Interrupted Ceremony

THE music began. Louise and Ken, arm in arm, began to skate around the pond, making long sweeps, first to the left, then to the right. When the circle was completed, they separated and did waltz jumps in unison.

Next came a pretty figure with the contestants swishing from side to side. Every few steps Ken lifted Louise from the ice. He swung her in an arc and she landed facing in the opposite direction. The audience clapped loudly.

The couple's footwork was flawless, and the crowd went wild as Louise and Ken separated and did an identical flip in perfect rhythm. The applause grew in volume as the pair, getting ready for their final figure, skated once more around the pond.

Jean knew what was coming and held her breath. Ken spun Louise about, then lifted her high above the ice. Jean's heart thumped. With his sore shoulder would he be able to keep from dropping Louise? Tensely Jean watched. Now Louise was lowered expertly, and the skaters went into the cartwheel lift, followed by a double jump.

"They did it!" Jean exclaimed excitedly. "They did it!"

The clapping and shouting lasted for a long time and no one was surprised when Louise and Ken were declared the winners of the figure-skating contest. The couple went to the table to receive their trophies, which were silver skating figures mounted on mahogany bases.

"That was an excellent performance," said Mr. Norton. "You two should continue as a skating pair and aim for the Olympics!"

Mrs. Crandall also congratulated them and the professor smiled broadly. The headmistress now announced that the pond would be cleared for the ceremony to crown the queen and her escort.

A buzz of excitement ran through the crowd as the man judge arose. "We have a request to make," he said over the loudspeaker. "Will each couple please skate once around the pond? Then we will choose the queen and her escort from among them."

One by one the pairs of skaters circled the pond, then lined up along the side nearest the school buildings to await the judges' selection.

The wait seemed interminable but finally a unanimous decision was handed to Mr. Norton. He read it, smiled, and spoke into the microphone.

"It gives me great pleasure to announce that the queen and her escort have been chosen for a splendid combination of form, technique, rhythm, and fine interpretation of the musical composition. The couple who have been chosen are—"

The athletic director's next words were drowned out by a horrible screeching yell from across the pond. Everyone looked in that direction and were horrified to see a huge, seven-foot tall, shaggy white-haired creature.

"The gorilla-man!" Louise gasped.

With unintelligible, piercing noises the monster headed directly for the bystanders who shrieked and fled in terror.

Lumbering up to the Crandalls, who stood transfixed, holding the robe and cape, the "gorilla" yanked them from their hands. Next, he knocked over the table and grabbed the golden paper crowns which he tore into pieces.

Urrhh! Urrhh! The ugly creature looked around menacingly. By this time the Danas and their dates had decided to take a hand before more damage was done.

"We must stop this monster!" cried Jean.

They rushed at the gorilla-man, but he lashed out at them with his long arms and great paws, making it difficult to get close to him. Still on skates, the four were at a disadvantage and it took several minutes of manoeuvring to surround the creature and finally seize him.

Quickly Ken yanked off the false head.

Revealed was a gawky youth who looked at them, terrified. "I—I give up!" he stammered. "D-don't hurt me!"

"What's the big idea?" Chris demanded as the Crandalls rushed over.

"It wasn't mine!" the young man blubbered. "I got paid for doing this—by a Starhurst girl!"

The professor was too stunned to speak. Mrs. Crandall's eyes opened wide. "You what!" she exclaimed incredulously.

"Who paid you?" Jean demanded.

The unmasked gorilla-man did not reply for several seconds, but seeing the angry faces of the six people around him, he finally burst out, "Lettie Briggs! She had me scare you in the woods the other day too!"

Everyone was astounded at this revelation except Louise and Jean, who had suspected Lettie of being involved in this mystery.

Louise turned to the shaggy-suited boy. "Is your name Charlie?"

"Yes. Please let me go—and make Miss Briggs pay for all this damage!"

Mrs. Crandall spoke up. "You will stay right here until we question Miss Briggs," she said crisply. At the moment the unpopular girl was not in sight.

By this time the other skaters were coming back, and the headmistress asked Doris Harland to find Lettie. Doris returned in a few minutes to say that Lettie was not around. "One of the maids told me she saw her go off in a taxi."

Mrs. Crandall frowned. The Danas guessed she was wondering what to do with Charlie. An answer came when Sam Gibbons, the detective-guard, hurried over. He had been patrolling in another part of the grounds.

"I think, Mr. Gibbons," said Mrs. Crandall, "you had better take this young man along and question him further."

Charlie, completely dejected, was led away. The queen's and escort's costumes were shaken out and once more held up by the headmistress and her husband.

The interruption had only temporarily dimmed the enthusiasm of the skaters and their audience. Now everyone listened attentively to Mr. Norton, who said:

"Our Starhurst skating queen and her escort are Louise Dana and Ken Scott!"

Amazed but thrilled, the pair skated forward. Both had fully expected that Marie Basler and Tommy Pitt would be chosen. Louise and Ken stood smiling while the robe and cape were adjusted in place, then skated down the pond amid cheers and hand clapping.

"I'm kind of glad Charlie ruined those crowns,"

said Ken under his breath. "I would have felt silly wearing one!" Louise chuckled.

As the couple came back to the shore, they were congratulated by the onlookers and skaters. Then the Starhurst girls gave their school cheer, which was followed by a rousing one from the Walton boys.

All the students and the visitors assembled in the big living room of the dormitory. Conversation was lively, and centered around the competition, the gorilla-man, and Lettie's disappearance.

The Danas looked around for Lettie's abandoned escort. He was seated at the piano. Apparently relieved of the company of the unpleasant girl, Jimmy Trask was now enjoying himself immensely. He played and sang several amusing songs. The Danas joined in the general laughter. That evening, at a formal dance which followed dinner, he had no difficulty finding partners.

When the festivities were over and Louise and Jean were getting ready for bed, Jean remarked, "What ails Lettie, anyhow? She's so silly to cheat herself out of good times."

Louise sighed. "Maybe someday she will learn."

The following morning Mrs. Crandall announced at breakfast that she had been in touch with Lettie's parents. Their daughter had come home because she was frightened at what Charlie had done. The girl insisted she had only paid the young man to put on entertainment for the students—not to frighten them. Charlie had worked at the Briggs' summer home in a town not far from Penfield. Lettie declared she had not asked Charlie to cause any damage or to interrupt the ceremony. The youth had since been dismissed by the police.

"We will forget the whole matter," said the headmistress in conclusion. "I request that when Lettie returns tomorrow, nothing be said to her about what happened."

Evelyn, who was seated next to Jean, remarked, "I hope Lettie has learned a lesson."

The episode was forgotten as the Starhurst girls dressed for chapel. The boys arrived in time to attend services with them. There was a midday dinner, followed by an old-fashioned sing, then the Walton group got ready to leave.

Chris grinned as he said good-bye to Jean. "Let's get together soon for some more barrel jumping."

"It's a date," she replied gaily.

Louise walked out to the waiting bus with Ken. "This has been a super week end," he told her. "And never forget, you are queen to this escort."

Louise smiled. "I like the title, even without a crown."

It was difficult for the girls to settle down to studies the next day. The understanding instructors did not ask their students any questions—instead, they did the talking with the girls taking notes.

The Danas and their friends were interested to note Lettie's subdued attitude. She hardly spoke to anyone and kept to herself. "Probably won't last long," Doris said wryly.

Louise and Jean, despite the fun and excitement of the week end, had not forgotten the mystery on which they were working, and that the fountain was to arrive by truck that evening. Jean asked Mrs. Crandall to let them know when it came.

"I'll send word to you immediately," the headmistress promised.

The sisters studied their homework diligently. They were not interrupted by any call. At nine-thirty Louise said to Jean, "Do you think Mrs. Crandall forgot?"

"I wonder. Let's go downstairs and find out about the fountain."

The girls went to the Crandalls' suite. Both the professor and his wife looked worried. "The truck has not arrived," said the elderly man. "It's strange that Mr. Mareno has not at least telephoned."

A feeling of alarm swept over the Danas. They did not show this, but suggested that the professor call Mr. Mareno's home.

He did so and learned to his dismay that the man's wife was greatly worried. Mr. Mareno and the trucker had gone to remove the fountain that afternoon. Neither she nor the trucker's wife had heard from their husbands since.

CHAPTER XIII

Valuable Ashes

"MAYBE Mr. Mareno and the trucker had an accident at the homestead!" Jean exclaimed. "Perhaps they're lying unconscious by the fountain!"

Louise suggested they go at once to find out. She urged Professor and Mrs. Crandall to drive there in the school car with the girls.

"Yes, right away!" the professor said. His former aversion to any publicity had to be put aside in light of the new events.

Mrs. Crandall, who had been deep in thought, now spoke up. "It is too dangerous for us to go without a police escort. I don't mind you girls trying to solve a mystery, but I must not let you run unnecessary risks."

She picked up her telephone and dialled police headquarters. The sergeant on duty was concerned when he heard the story of the missing men and promised to send officers to investigate at once.

"Professor Crandall and I and two of our students wish to go with them," the headmistress said. "My husband owns that fountain."

The sergeant consented, and within fifteen minutes officers McGuire and Kane, who were on night duty, arrived at the school.

Kane said he had been amazed to hear about the missing men. "I was out at the old place myself when I came on duty this afternoon. Mareno and his friend were at the fountain with hoisting equipment. They were getting ready to work. One hour later I stopped there again."

"Did you see the men?" Jean asked eagerly.

The officer shook his head. "The frozen fountain was there, but the men were gone, and so was the truck. I assumed they were having difficulty and left to pick up more equipment."

Louise was impatient to be off. "We'd better hurry over there and find out what we can," she urged, and the officers agreed.

The headmistress, her husband, and the Danas got into the station wagon and followed the policemen to the Price homestead. Louise and Jean led the way up the front walk, then to the right down a path to the garden. The group played flashlights over the wintry scene.

"The fountain is still here!" Professor Crandall exclaimed. "Thank goodness!"

The police, together with the Danas, made a thorough search of the area. Scrambled, confused marks in the snow clearly indicated a struggle of some kind had taken place.

"From the footprints, I'd say several people were involved," McGuire remarked.

The four from Starhurst were now doubly alarmed. Jean expressed their fears. "Mr. Mareno and his helper must have been abducted!"

"But why?" Mrs. Crandall asked. "They had absolutely nothing to do with the mystery except to move the fountain."

Louise had a ready answer. "They would tell of the attack and identify the person or persons responsible."

She suggested that they look in the deserted house. "The men may be in there, and if not, we might find a clue to their attackers."

The two officers held a consultation, then said it was a good idea but they would have to summon Mr. Black, who had the key. Officer Kane went out to the patrol car and radioed headquarters. He was told that the agent would be brought to the homestead.

When he arrived, Mr. Black unlocked the front door and the whole group entered the cold house. Flashlights were played into every one of the first-floor rooms. No one was there, so the two officers went upstairs to investigate.

While they were gone, Louise and Jean made a discovery. Ashes in the living-room fireplace were slightly warm, proving that someone had used the place not many hours before.

"I guess the men in the police car didn't notice the smoke," said Louise.

"And there are some scraps of food on the floor," Jean pointed out. "I'll bet Mr. Mareno and his friend were prisoners here until it got dark and it was safe for the abductors to take them away."

"Oh, dear!" Professor Crandall sighed. "I seem to have involved so many people in what has developed into real trouble. It might have been better if I had not admired the Cellini fountain so much I felt I had to own it."

Mrs. Crandall gave her husband a sideways glance as if she agreed, but she merely said, "The important thing now is to find the missing men. Do you realize what this means? One or more very dangerous characters are at large in our area. The thought frightens me when I realize how many young ladies my husband and I must protect."

At that moment the two officers came downstairs and announced that they had investigated the second and third floors and found no clues. The cellar door was still bolted, so no one could be hiding there.

Jean had a sudden thought. "We were told the other day that some criminals headed for Chicago were in this section. Do you think the abductors could be part of that gang?"

"It's possible," Officer McGuire replied. "But we have searched Penfield and the area around it very thoroughly and found no clues to any wanted criminal except Red Shanley. I doubt he would resort to abduction."

Jean announced her discovery of the warm ashes and the scraps of food. The policemen raised their eyebrows. Officer Kane said, "I will report this at once to headquarters."

Mr. Black had been silent all this while and kept pacing up and down nervously. Officer McGuire turned to him and was about to speak, when Louise cried out:

"I see something!" She rushed over to the fireplace, leaned down, and plucked a gleaming object from the ashes. "A diamond!" she exclaimed.

The others dashed to Louise's side. She blew the ashes from the stone and rubbed it against her coat to clean it. She held the gem in front of Officer McGuire's flashlight. Its sparkling surfaces picked up the various colours of the clothing worn by the group.

"It certainly looks genuine," the officer said. "But how in the world did a diamond get into the fireplace?"

Officer McGuire felt that the gem might have been dropped by one of the abductors, and Kane theorized, "It may not have been set in a piece of jewelry, but been a loose stone—perhaps stolen— and it fell out of the thief's pocket."

Louise asked, "Do you think perhaps the diamond belongs to a woman who is involved with the gang? Maybe she's the wife of one of the members?"

The policemen nodded and Officer McGuire said he would take the stone to headquarters.

At this point, Mr. Black spoke up for the first time. "I'd say that anything found in the house should be turned over to me. After all, I'm in charge until the new owners move in."

He was overruled by the officers who said that the diamond would be marked for identification and be listed as having come from the homestead.

"There's nothing more we can do here," Kane said, and the group filed outside.

When they reached the school, the Danas realized that it was long after lights-out time. They went quietly to their suite. As they got ready for bed, they discussed in whispers the possible abduction. The mystery certainly was becoming more complicated.

Both girls were fearful that despite the police checking into the Price grounds, the mysterious people who were tampering with the fountain and using the house without permission might yet succeed in removing the fountain.

"Two questions keep puzzling me," said Louise. "Are there two gangs—one apparently trying to steal the fountain, the other insisting that it stay?

Or do you suppose there's just a single gang, with one faction trying to double-cross the other?"

Jean yawned. "I've used my brain so hard today I can't think up another reason for anything. Good night, Sis. Pleasant dreams. See you in the morning!"

The girls slept soundly but were awake early. "It's a beautiful bright morning!" Louise said as she looked out the window. "Jean, let's take a quick walk before breakfast."

The girls hurriedly dressed and found that they had about fifteen minutes before the bell would ring. They went outdoors and walked briskly along a path.

Suddenly Jean said, "I'll race you across the lawn to the front gate!"

"I'm game."

The two girls started running side by side, but in a few seconds Jean began to pull ahead. She dashed wildly through the snow, turning her head to laugh at her sister. A moment later Jean cried out in pain and fell.

"Oh, oh!" she wailed.

Louise rushed to her side. "What's the matter? What happened?"

She started to help Jean up.

"Oh, be careful!" her sister begged. "I stepped in a hole. I think I've sprained my ankle!"

CHAPTER XIV

Attic Search

LOUISE lifted her sister from the snow and told her to put an arm around her neck. With Jean hopping along, the twosome made their way back to the dormitory.

"We'd better go right to the infirmary," Louise said. "I can see that your ankle is already swelling."

At that moment Professor and Mrs. Crandall appeared in the hall and inquired what had happened.

"I've sprained my ankle, I guess," said Jean. "I was running across the lawn, and stepped in a hole."

The professor was deeply disturbed. "Oh, dear! Oh, dear!" he said. "I'm afraid that's my fault."

"Your fault?" Louise echoed.

The elderly man explained that he had called in a retired well-digger from Penfield who said he could locate springs for the fountain. The man had dug in several places on the Starhurst grounds, but up to the moment had not found water.

"The recent snow covered the holes before he could fill them in," said the professor. "I should have realized the danger."

He apologized profusely to Jean for not having warned the faculty and students to be careful while crossing the lawn. His wife said she would make the announcement at breakfast.

"I shall call the doctor at once to examine your ankle and foot, Jean," the headmistress said. "Can you girls manage to get up to the infirmary without other assistance?"

"I'll help," Professor Crandall offered.

He stepped alongside Jean and told her to put her free arm about his neck. Slowly the three climbed to the third floor and entered the infirmary office. Miss Pilling, the school nurse, greeted them and asked about the accident. As Jean was explaining, the professor left.

Louise said Dr. Malcolm was coming. The nurse suggested that Jean lie down while waiting for him. The physician arrived in a few minutes, and after a thorough examination, said that Jean had indeed sprained her ankle.

"You'll have to stay in bed for two or three days, young lady."

Jean groaned. "That long?" she said woefully. "Dr. Malcolm, my sister and I have a mystery to solve."

The kindly, jovial man smiled. "I am afraid, my dear, that you will have to do your sleuthing from this infirmary."

Jean made a wry face, but suddenly her eyes lighted up. "I'll do just that!"

She had just been made comfortable in one of the beds when Louise heard the breakfast bell ring. She said good-bye to her sister, hurried down to her room, and quickly removed her wraps. As Louise hustled along the hallway to the front stairs, she met Doris and Evelyn.

"Where's Jean?" Doris asked cheerfully. Louise explained what had happened.

"That's a shame!" Doris and Evelyn cried together.

The story was repeated by Mrs. Crandall during the breakfast hour. "All students, please be extra careful walking in that area. I will have markers placed over the holes to warn you."

Evelyn was unusually silent during the meal. When it was over, she said to Louise, "I'd like to go up and see Jean. Will you come? I have an idea."

"Oh, yes," Louise said. "We'll hurry through our room chores. That'll give us a chance for a visit before our first class."

When the two girls reached the infirmary, Jean's ankle was bandaged and she was sitting up in bed. Her face brightened at seeing the girls.

Evelyn told her how sorry she was, then added, "I have a plan for trying to find a spring."

"That will certainly please Professor Crandall," Jean remarked. "What do you have in mind?"

Evelyn went on to say that when her family had sold the estate to be used as Starhurst School, they had had to leave trunks containing various articles behind. "They're in the loft of the barn which is now the garage. I have a vague recollection of an old map of these grounds on which a bubbling spring was marked."

The Danas were interested to hear this. Louise said, "And you think the map might be in one of the trunks?"

Evelyn nodded. "I want to look through them this afternoon after classes. Louise, will you help me?"

"I'd love to," Louise answered.

"Good. Oh, by the way, any news about Mr. Mareno and his friend?"

Louise replied somberly, "We haven't heard a word from the police."

"Anyhow," Jean put in hopefully, "by the time Professor Crandall *does* get that fountain over here, you two will have solved the problem of the water."

Louise and Evelyn now stood up to leave, and told Jean to take it easy.

"I'll have to." Jean sighed. "But I can't just stay in this bed and idle my time away! Louise, will you bring my books up here? At least I can keep up with my studies."

Louise chuckled. "I thought you were going to concentrate on the mystery and solve it."

Jean grinned. "What makes you think I can't do both?"

Her sister hurried off and returned in a few minutes with an armful of books, a note pad, and a pencil. Then she herself hurried off to her first class. That afternoon Louise and Evelyn put on old clothes and walked across the campus to the barn-garage.

Up in the cluttered loft, Evelyn hardly knew where to start. Finally she chose the largest trunk. As she unfastened the clasp and lifted the lid, the girls heard footsteps on the stairway. They turned to see who was coming and in a moment Lettie Briggs appeared.

"Hi!" she called cheerfully. "What are you two doing?"

Neither Louise nor Evelyn had any intention of telling the inquisitive girl, and they merely said hello.

Lettie shrugged. "Okay, don't tell me. I intend to stay here and see what you're up to. Remember, I have just as many privileges at Starhurst as you two. I have a right to know what's going on any place on the school grounds."

Louise and Evelyn ignored her pronouncement. Evelyn was about to lift up a stack of old letters when she turned to face the unwelcome visitor. "I'll make a bargain with you, Lettie," she said.

"You tell us who took the riddle off Louise's desk, and I'll tell you what we're hunting for."

Apparently Lettie could not think of what to say. Her hesitation seemed to imply an admission of guilt about the disappearance of the riddle. Finally Lettie said, "What makes you think I know who took your old paper? If that's your bargain, I'm not falling for it. But I'm still staying here."

Nothing more was said. Louise and Evelyn worked quietly, looking through stacks of papers. They came across many interesting items concerning the settlement of Starhurst by its original owner, but there was no clue to the old map they were seeking.

Lettie had become more and more curious, but she did not dare hover too close to the girls for fear they would stop their search. After a while they forgot she was there. By now they were working in different areas of the attic. Presently Louise untied a bundle of yellowed papers. Among them was a hand-drawn map.

"Evelyn, I think I've found it!" she exclaimed.

Not only Evelyn, but Lettie as well, dashed to Louise's side. Suddenly Lettie's toe rammed into a loosened floor board and she went sprawling. In trying to save herself, she grabbed at the corner of a tall box. It tilted and fell on her back.

Lettie screamed. Louise and Evelyn rushed to her. Quickly they lifted the box away and helped Lettie to her feet.

"Oh, my back is broken!" she cried out. "And it's all your fault!"

"I'm sorry this happened," said Louise, "but we certainly had nothing to do with it. Come. We'll help you to the infirmary. Try walking and see if your back hurts too much."

Lettie was able to walk, but did look white and shaken. Louise and Evelyn assisted her to the foot of the stairs. There she declared she could not take another step, so the others made a chair seat of their hands. Lettie, complaining constantly, was carried to the dormitory.

Several students saw the girls coming and crowded around. Louise asked one of them to go to the infirmary for a stretcher. When it appeared, with Miss Pilling in charge, willing hands transported Lettie to the third floor. Once more Dr. Malcolm was summoned. He reported later that Lettie had sustained some nasty bruises but no serious injury to her back. She was to stay in the infirmary until the soreness was gone.

"Poor Jean!" murmured Evelyn.

She and Louise went back to their search. The map which Louise had found contained no information about a spring. The hunt continued.

Half an hour later, Evelyn exclaimed excitedly, "I've found half the map! I don't see the other part."

Louise went to look at it. The paper was fragile with age, and the figures and writing on it dim. The girls scrutinized every bit of the map carefully and finally concluded that no spring was marked on this half.

"The notation must be on the missing part," Evelyn concluded. "It's too late for us to continue searching today. But I'm determined to find the rest of this map!"

The two girls returned to the dormitory. Louise went to Mrs. Crandall's apartment to ask if any call had come from the police about the kidnapped men. When she learned that none had, Louise asked permission to call headquarters.

"Go ahead. I want to hear the latest news myself," the headmistress said.

Louise spoke to Captain James, who said that every lead had been followed but with no results. Furthermore, there was no evidence that anyone had been at the homestead or near the fountain since the search of the previous day.

"Any clues about that diamond?" Louise asked.

In reply the captain said mysteriously, "Look in this morning's *Penfield Post*."

CHAPTER XV

Police-File Clue

AFTER saying good-bye to the police captain, Louise asked Mrs. Crandall if she might look at the morning newspaper. She and the headmistress scanned it quickly. No headline or caption gave a clue to explain the officer's remark about the diamond Louise had found in the Price fireplace.

Finally Louise asked, "May I take the paper up to the infirmary and go over it more carefully with Jean?"

"Yes, but please bring it back when you've finished."

Louise took the two flights of steps at a run and hurried into Jean's infirmary room. She explained to Jean that the captain had urged her to look in the morning paper.

"I didn't see anything in the headlines, but maybe it's in the fine print," she said.

The sisters put their heads together and looked at

every word of every column. Finally nothing was left but the "Lost and Found" column. They started reading each notice meticulously.

"Here's something!" Jean said, as she came to the item:

LOST: *Solitaire diamond. Write Box PG 49* Penfield Post.

"Do you suppose this is what Captain James meant?" Louise asked. "I believe it is, and he didn't want to discuss the ad on the phone."

Jean agreed. "Why don't you go immediately to headquarters and talk to the captain?"

"Good idea," Louise said. "I'll ask Professor Crandall to drive me down."

"I certainly wish I could go with you," Jean murmured. "Oh, why did I have to sprain an ankle!"

Louise patted her sister on the shoulder and promised to tell her what she found out as soon as she returned to Starhurst. Louise took the paper with her and gave it to Mrs. Crandall, pointing out the item in the "Lost and Found" column.

"*Hmm,*" said the headmistress with a slight smile. "I suppose you'd like to go right down to headquarters."

Louise laughed. "You read my mind, Mrs. Crandall."

The professor came in at that moment. He gladly assented to drive Louise to headquarters. Upon their arrival Captain James took them into his private office. A twinkle in his eye, he praised the Danas for finding the item to which he had referred.

"The police have a plan for trying to identify the person who put the ad in the paper. We have a policewoman working with us, who, so far as anyone else knows, has no connection with the police department. She has answered the ad from her home."

"Has she had a reply yet?" Louise asked.

"No," the captain answered, "but we expect she will soon. I'll phone you when we receive more information."

Louise was delighted with the arrangement, and Professor Crandall remarked, "I hope this may prove to be the beginning of a break in the case."

The officer went on to say that there was still no news of Mr. Mareno and his trucker friend. There had been no ransom note or demands of any kind on the men's families.

"It is a most unusual abduction case," Captain James remarked, "and both men's wives are in a state of shock."

"I'm terribly sorry to hear that," Louise said. "But I can hardly blame them."

The captain told his callers he must say good-by, as he had another appointment. Before leaving, Louise asked him if she might look through the police files for the record on Red Shanley, the forger.

"Certainly." The captain summoned a guard who led Louise and Professor Crandall to the file room. Finding the right drawer, Louise flipped through the S folders until she came to one marked: SHANLEY, Thomas (nickname Red).

"Read the data to me," Professor Crandall requested, and she began.

Red Shanley had been a wayward youth, constantly in and out of reformatories.

"Then he apparently reformed for a while. He married, and eventually became a professional skater—" Louise stopped abruptly.

Her mind suddenly flew to the phantom skaters on the Starhurst pond. Could Red have been one of them? His fingerprints *had* been found in the Price homestead and the phantom skaters had certainly performed like professionals!

"Go on," Professor Crandall urged. "Did he stay out of prison?"

"Apparently, yes," Louise replied, reading further. "But he was caught forging a cheque. It says here Shanley avoided prosecution, but he was blackballed as a professional skater."

The professor asked, "Didn't the police say he's wanted as a forger?"

"That's right," Louise agreed. "Maybe it will tell here why."

She read on and learned that Shanley had forged a large cheque to pay a hotel bill at a summer resort. He had vanished from the place and not been heard of since. The first clue to Red's whereabouts had come when his fingerprints had been found in the Price homestead. The record ended with the statement that the police had been unable to find any other trace of him.

Louise closed the drawer of the file and walked out to the main room with the professor. She went up to the sergeant on duty and revealed her suspicions about the phantom skaters. "One might have been Red Shanley, the other his wife," she suggested.

"Thank you for the tip, Miss Dana," he said. "We'll pass along the word."

"In case he hasn't left Penfield," said Louise, "it's possible he may come back at night and skate on our school pond."

The sergeant smiled. "You could be right. I'll tell the captain. Maybe he'll want to send a couple of men out there to watch—if they can be spared."

Louise thanked the sergeant for the opportunity of looking at the files, then she and the professor returned to Starhurst. The young sleuth could not get the idea out of her mind that the wanted forger had a skeleton key to the Price homestead.

"Shanley might even have something to do with Mr. Mareno's kidnapping," Louise thought.

She went directly to the infirmary and talked with her sister. "You certainly learned a lot," Jean commented. "Oh, I wish I could have been with you!"

Louise said she wanted to go out to the homestead and see if she could find any more clues. "I'll get a group together tomorrow."

The following day Louise made arrangements, and after classes she, Evelyn, and Doris trekked there with Mr. Black and Professor Crandall. Police officers McGuire and Kane, now on the day shift, met them at the fountain. The girls and the professor heaved sighs of relief to see the fountain still in place. It was tipped over still farther, however.

"Someone's been digging at the base again!" Louise exclaimed.

The group examined the foundation carefully and Evelyn exclaimed in dismay, "The fountain could be carted off easily now!"

The two policemen looked at each other. Noting fresh footprints, Officer McGuire said, "You girls stay here while we men inspect the house. It may be dangerous in there if anyone is around."

The three girls continued to examine the frozen fountain. There was no evidence of further attempts to chip off the ice, and the beautiful piece with its dancing nymphs was still intact.

Louise said with a sigh, "If I weren't afraid of marring the fountain, I'd say a whole group of us girls could put ropes around it now and drag the piece to Starhurst!"

Suddenly a guttural voice behind them thundered, "You will never take that fountain anywhere!"

The girls turned. Striding toward them with great steps was the white, shaggy-furred gorilla-man! He was swinging a club menacingly in his huge right hand.

The girls began to laugh uproariously. Their amusement seemed to infuriate the creature, who growled and swung his club back and forth with great force.

Louise said calmly, "Charlie, you can't fool us twice!"

By now the gorilla-man was only a few feet from them. He boomed out, "I am not Charlie! You have been warned to stay away from here! This fountain belongs to me! It's mine! Don't you touch it!"

Suddenly the girls realized that the masquerader was not Charlie. The person inside the shaggy white suit was a much bigger man than Charlie. Also, the costume was somewhat different from the one worn by the youth. This man was not just a mischief-maker. He meant business with the swinging club!

CHAPTER XVI

Candies and Costumes

WHEN Doris realized the danger confronting the girls from the mysterious gorilla-man, she shrieked and ran toward the homestead. Louise and Evelyn decided not to argue with the club-swinging stranger, and to follow Doris.

Reaching the house, they pounded on the front door and Doris cried out, "Let us in! We're in danger!"

The door was opened by Officer McGuire. Doris gasped out, "Another gorilla-man! This one has a big club! He threatened us!"

"Where is he?" the officer asked.

"At the fountain."

By this time Officer Kane had appeared and together the two men ran down the path that led to the garden.

"I want to find out who that gorilla-man is!" Louise said, and started down the steps.

Doris and Evelyn held her back. Evelyn said, "We won't let you. It's too dangerous."

"I suppose you're right," Louise conceded. She turned, and followed her friends into the house. Professor Crandall and Mr. Black were told what had just happened. Both men were astounded and the professor looked worried.

"I hope the police capture him," he said. "I believe he is the one who is trying to steal the fountain."

Five minutes passed. Louise could not stand the strain of waiting any longer and went outdoors. McGuire and Kane were coming up the front walk.

"Did you catch him?" Louise asked.

McGuire shook his head. "He had too much of a head start. But we got a clue to his identity. We followed his big, flat prints for some distance. Then apparently he shed his costume and went on to the street."

"You mean," said Louise, "from that point there's another set of prints?"

"Yes," Kane replied. "The second set were made by large-sized boots."

On a hunch Louise asked, "Are there three parallel marks across the sole?"

The officer looked at her in amazement. "Yes. How do you know that?"

Louise had a startling answer. She said, "I believe that gorilla-man has another disguise—he is also masquerading as the blond woman! He wears a wig."

Officer McGuire looked intently at the young sleuth. "That's an amazing deduction," he said in admiration. "This is certainly a big step in putting the pieces of this puzzling mystery together."

Kane nodded. "It might also explain why we police haven't seen the blonde around. This character has used the woman disguise while stalking these woods and trying to steal the fountain. No doubt he found out the police were looking for a big blond woman, and went back to appearing as a man. But if he's a wanted criminal, he probably is using other disguises."

Louise went into the house with the officers and told the others the latest findings. Professor Crandall was very upset over the whole episode, so Louise suggested that the Starhurst group return to school. They said good-bye to Mr. Black and the officers and set off.

As they trudged through the snowy woods, Evelyn and Doris pleaded with the professor to have the fountain removed at once. He promised to attend to the matter immediately.

Louise said little. She was toying with an idea which might give her a clue to the identity of the man who played the part of a blond woman. "I believe Lettie can help me," she thought.

Back at the dormitory, Louise learned that Lettie

had left the infirmary and was now in her room. The young sleuth went directly there. "How are you feeling?" she asked Lettie.

Was it Louise's imagination or did the girl seem subdued? Her reply was quiet and sincere.

"I'm better, thank you," she said. "You probably think me a pretty poor sport blaming my accident on you and then never thanking you and Evelyn for carrying me back here."

Louise, who had grown used to Lettie's bombastic outbursts, was so amazed at the girl's attitude she hardly knew how to answer her. Finally Louise said, "We were glad to help. I'm only sorry you got hurt."

Lettie admitted it was her own fault and that it had not been very nice of her to be so curious. She managed a faint smile. "But I would like to know how you're making out with the mystery."

When Louise told her about the second gorilla-man, Lettie gasped. "He must have gotten the idea from seeing Charlie."

Louise agreed that perhaps the stranger had. She then told of her suspicion that the gorilla-man was actually the big blond woman who had grabbed hold of Lettie.

"What!"

Louise said that if Lettie wanted to help clear up the mystery there was a way she might do it.

"How?"

"It's just possible," Louise went on, "that this

second gorilla-man rented or purchased his costume from the same place Charlie did. Do you know where that is?"

Lettie did not answer at once. Finally she said, "You understand I don't know anything about the second gorilla-man, but I will tell you where Charlie rented his costume. I told you I was on my way to get some maple syrup and candy for my parents the day that blonde grabbed me. That was true. They're made and sold at a house over on Beechcroft Road by Mr. and Mrs. Rymer. They also make and rent costumes."

Lettie paused, then asked, "Promise me one thing. I don't want Charlie to get into any trouble —he's really a nice boy but kind of dumb. Please don't tell the police where he got the costume or they may accuse him of being in league with the other gorilla-man."

Louise promised not to give any hint of a connection between the two. She thanked Lettie for the information, then ran to the infirmary to see Jean. Her sister was feeling much better and chafing to return to full activity. Suddenly Jean smiled enigmatically. "I'm working on something in connection with the mystery. I think I may have a good clue. But in case I'm wrong, I'm not going to tell you about it yet."

Louise grinned. "I can't wait." Then she briefed Jean on the afternoon's adventures and Lettie's helpfulness.

Jean gaped in astonishment. "Lettie cooperating! I can hardly believe it!"

Her sister arose. "I want to investigate that candy-and-costume place. See you soon."

Louise hurried downstairs and asked Professor and Mrs. Crandall to take her to the Rymers' shop.

"Why don't we let the police check?" the headmistress suggested.

Louise recalled her promise to Lettie. "Oh, please, let's not tell them yet," she begged. "At least, not until we've questioned the Rymers."

"All right," Mrs. Crandall said. "We will take you to the shop." She looked at her wristwatch. "We'd better go right away because they'll probably close within a half hour."

Mr. and Mrs. Rymer were an elderly couple, who were very friendly and talkative. They admitted having rented a gorilla costume to a young man by the name of Charlie Davis.

"He ruined the outfit," said Mrs. Rymer, "but he did pay for it. Somebody gave him the money."

Louise was sure that the person was Lettie. She asked, "Did anyone else come here to rent a similar costume?"

"Why, yes," Mr. Rymer said. "A tall, blond woman named Mrs. Stevenson ordered one. She said she wanted it to fit her, but it should resemble as nearly as possible the one Charlie had."

Louise smiled. "You did a very good job. We

saw both costumes and they surely did look alike. Have you any idea where Mrs. Stevenson was going to wear the suit?"

After thinking over the question a moment, Mr. Rymer answered. "Come to think of it, she didn't say. We assumed it was for some fancy-dress party."

"Does Mrs. Stevenson live in Penfield?" Louise questioned.

"Seems to me she said she was staying in town," Mr. Rymer replied, "but I got the impression she doesn't live here all the time."

Louise and the Crandalls bought some maple syrup and candy, and the headmistress said she would be back to purchase more for the school.

As the callers were about to leave, Mrs. Rymer said, "By the way, one of your students ordered a costume from us for a school skating party. She never came for the Snow Queen outfit. Maybe you'd like to take it to her."

Mrs. Crandall said the skating affair was over so the costume would not be needed. But Louise asked quickly, "Who was the student?"

"Miss Briggs."

Two ideas suddenly flashed into Louise's mind. Apparently Lettie had been afraid to go through the woods and pick up the costume and had purchased another one in Penfield.

Also, Louise thought, if Lettie did not continue her seemingly reformed behavior, the outfit would lend itself to a wonderful joke. She turned to Mrs. Crandall. "If you don't mind, I'd like to take the costume to Lettie, anyway. How much does it cost to rent, Mrs. Rymer?"

"Oh, Miss Briggs has already paid us."

Hearing this, Mrs. Crandall agreed to Louise's request. Mrs. Rymer went into a back room and brought out the costume.

"How beautiful!" Louise exclaimed as she gazed at a long, flowing white dress and mask and gold crown.

A different theory now occurred to Louise about Lettie's reason for ordering the Snow Queen costume. "I believe she planned to use it for some kind of trick," thought Louise. "Maybe she was going to put on a 'show' with Charlie, but when she got a date, Lettie decided not to go through with her idea."

The Crandalls did not detect the mischievous look in Louise's eyes as she thought about a way to deliver the white costume to Lettie.

"I'll wait and see if she has really reformed!" Louise decided.

As she and the Crandalls drove back toward the school, Louise asked the professor to stop for a moment at headquarters. She wanted to tell the police about "Mrs. Stevenson."

Captain James was just about to leave but stopped to greet Louise. She quickly told him the big blond "woman" called herself Mrs. Stevenson. "I found out from the Rymers that she had a gorilla costume made for herself. Also, she has been staying in Penfield."

The officer lifted his eyebrows. "This is a vital piece of information," he said. "You have certainly done an excellent job, Miss Dana."

The girl blushed at his praise.

"And now I have some information for you," the captain said. "About half an hour ago our policewoman had a phoned response to her letter in answer to the newspaper ad."

"Who called?" Louise asked excitedly.

"A woman who said she was Mrs. Stevenson!"

CHAPTER XVII

A Ghost Speaks

"Mrs. Stevenson!" Louise echoed in surprise. "The alias of the phony blond woman!" Eagerly she asked what the police planned to do next.

"We'll have stake-outs at the home of our police-woman," Captain James replied. "I'll tell you our suspicions about this diamond mystery. Please keep it confidential, except from Professor and Mrs. Crandall and your sister."

"I will."

The officer said that a very valuable diamond ring had disappeared from the local jewelry shop of Max Richter. The police thought the diamond which Louise had found might be the missing gem, removed from the gold band. "Mr. Richter has weighed the stone and says it is the same weight and cut as the stolen one."

"Was anything else taken from the shop?" Louise asked.

"Several pieces of jewellery," the captain responded.

He told Louise that at the present time not only Richter's, but the fine jewellery sections of the two large department stores in Penfield were being watched for more thefts.

The officer again thanked Louise for all her help and said he would be in touch with her or with the Crandalls the moment there was any further word on any aspects of the mysteries.

As soon as Louise seated herself in the car she relayed the information to the headmistress and her husband. The professor rubbed his head. "Things are moving so fast I'm dizzy," he said. "And we seem to become more and more involved with criminals."

Mrs. Crandall conceded this was true and remarked that she had the reputation of Starhurst and the girls' safety to guard. "We cannot become too deeply implicated," she said.

For a moment Louise was fearful the privilege of helping Professor Crandall solve the fountain mystery might be withdrawn. But the headmistress said nothing more and presently they arrived at the school.

Before dinner, Louise hurried to the infirmary to report again to her sister. "Your news is astounding!" Jean said. "Oh, I hope the Mrs. Stevenson who's going to the policewoman's house is the same one we're looking for."

Louise smiled. "I have a hunch she is."

Then Louise told about Lettie, her seeming change of heart, and the Snow Queen costume.

Jean grinned. "I hate to be suspicious, but if Lettie Briggs has reformed, I'll think the world is coming to an end!"

A bell rang and Louise said, "I must go, Jean. Be seeing you."

After dinner Louise immediately tackled her homework. She had missed the chance to do any that afternoon and had a special English assignment which she knew would take at least an hour. The English instructor had handed each girl in the class a lengthy list of instructions for a theme. Each student had received a different list and the themes were to be exchanged for criticism.

Louise opened her notebook to get out the list. It was not there. She held the book up and shook it. Nothing fell out. Perplexed, she looked through her other books and papers, on top of the desk, and finally in each drawer. The assignment paper was not to be found.

"But what could have happened to it?" she asked herself. "It was right here. I read through the list quickly after I put my books down."

No one would have borrowed the paper, she knew, because each assignment was different. Suddenly it occurred to Louise that maybe Lettie's reform had not been sincere and that she was playing another trick. She knew it would do no good to ask the girl, so she went to Evelyn's room and told her about the missing paper.

"Did you see either Lettie or Ina go into my room?" Louise asked. "Ina knew about the assignments, and she might have told Lettie."

Evelyn made a gesture like a salute. "You've probably guessed the answer, detective," she said. "While you were away this afternoon, I did see Lettie come out of your room. There wasn't anything in her hand, but she could have tucked the paper under her sweater. Do you think she'll give it back if you ask her?"

Louise chuckled. "I'm not going to give her the satisfaction. Fortunately, I remember the important points of the assignment. But I'll let you in on a little secret. After the lights-out room check tonight, open your door a crack and watch." Louise would say no more.

She went back to her own room and had just finished her homework when the bell for the end of study hour sounded.

Louise hurried upstairs to the infirmary to say good night to Jean and tell of her suspicions about Lettie's latest prank.

"I've a plan for finding out if she's responsible. After lights-out check, I'm going to put on the Snow Queen costume, and float like a ghost into Lettie's room!"

Jean giggled merrily, wishing Louise luck. "Let me know what happens!"

Meanwhile, Evelyn had passed the word to several friends along the corridor to watch for an interesting show. Half an hour later all the room lights were out and the monitor came around to see that everyone was in bed. Louise feigned sleep.

Five minutes later she was up and slipping the Snow Queen costume over her pyjamas. She pinned on the crown and adjusted the mask. Then quietly she went into the hall. Various doors had opened a few inches and inquisitive eyes peered out. The "queen" waved at them as she went along.

In a few moments Louise reached Lettie and Ina's room. Quietly she opened the door, gave a moaning sound, and glided in. Ina shrieked and dived under the covers. Lettie sat bolt upright and stared at the figure in white. The light was very dim, but Louise thought she detected a look of terror on the girl's face.

The ghostly queen pointed a finger at Lettie and said in a deep, hollow voice, "You have committed many misdeeds, including taking papers from students' rooms. You must atone for them or grave punishment will come to you!"

Louise glided closer to the bed. "Lettie Briggs, do you promise to atone?"

"I do! I do!" Lettie wailed.

"Get under the covers!" the Snow Queen ordered. "Start thinking how you will make amends!"

Lettie did as she was told. Louise removed the

costume, mask, and crown and laid them on a chair. Then she vanished from the room, closing the door softly and quickly.

Putting a finger to her lips to warn the onlookers not to burst into giggles, Louise made her way speedily back to her own room and got into bed. She went to sleep with a wide grin on her face.

At breakfast the group who had witnessed Louise's joke gave no sign that they knew anything about it. Louise in turn gave no indication to Lettie, merely saying, "Good morning. How is your back?"

Lettie gave Louise a black look. "It's okay."

Mrs. Crandall arose presently to make her usual morning announcements. The last one was: "Will Louise Dana please come to the office directly after breakfast."

Louise was excited. Had Mrs. Stevenson been captured?

When she arrived at the office, Professor Crandall was there. He told Louise he had had an early telephone call from the police. "The truck belonging to Mr. Mareno's friend has been found abandoned several miles from here."

"What about the kidnapped men?" Louise asked him.

"No clue to their whereabouts."

The elderly man added that the whole area around Waynesboro where the truck had been found had been thoroughly investigated—houses, barns, garages, and other buildings. "The police did not dig up a single clue to any hiding place, and they believe that the men may have been taken a great distance from here."

"What are the police going to do now?" Louise put in.

The professor said that they seemed to be stymied. A three-state alarm had been sent out and many leads had been followed but to no avail.

Louise's heart sank at this turn of events. She asked how Mrs. Mareno and the trucker's wife were bearing up.

"I understand both of them are under doctors' care," the professor answered. He began to pace the floor. "I feel responsible for all this. Oh, if only something could be done!"

"There's bound to be a break in the case," Louise said encouragingly. But secretly she was extremely discouraged and fearful. The kidnappers might have harmed Mr. Mareno and his friend. They might never be seen again!

"I will let you know if I receive any further information," the professor promised.

That afternoon, when Louise returned from classes to her room, Jean came limping in.

"I've been discharged from the infirmary!" she said.

"Wonderful!" Louise hugged her sister.

Jean sat down on Louise's bed. Her face wore an excited expression. "Louise," she said, "I think I've figured out part of that riddle we received in the mail."

"Really? Tell me!"

Jean said first she wanted to check with Starhurst's teacher of Italian. "Give me a hand and we'll go find Miss Paglio."

As the Danas went down the hall toward the stairway, Louise pleaded, "Please brief me on your idea."

Jean, a mischievous look in her eyes, said, "Not yet. But I'll tell you one thing: I believe the clue to the riddle is in the word 'welcome.'"

CHAPTER XVIII

The Diamond Trap

THE Danas found Miss Paglio in the Starhurst library. She smiled at them.

Jean asked her, "Miss Paglio, what is the Italian word for welcome?"

"It is *benvenuto*."

Excitement danced in Jean's eyes. "That's Cellini's first name—Benvenuto!"

"Correct."

"Thank you so much," Jean said hastily, and rushed her sister from the library. Out in the hallway, Jean whispered excitedly, "Do you know what this means, Louise? You remember that line in the riddle: 'Walk to the welcome spot'? The initials B. C. could stand for Benvenuto Cellini. And the message could mean: Walk to the Cellini spot—that's the fountain!"

"That's real sleuthing," Louise said. "How in the world did you ever figure that out?"

Jean laughed. "Didn't I tell you I'd work on the mystery while I was in the infirmary?" Then she became serious. "I've thought of that riddle over and over again. Each time I said it, the word 'welcome' seemed to stand out. It's out óf context to the other lines, so I wondered if it had some special significance. French and German translations of the word meant nothing. I thought I'd see what it is in Italian."

Louise now was grinning from ear to ear. "You are a real genius, Sis. And you've put my brain to work too. Remember the line 'Look to your right'? If you walk down the garden path from the homestead, the fountain stands on your right."

Jean said she had mulled over this too. "Maybe something important is buried near the fountain."

Louise nodded. "If so, what? And the biggest puzzle of all, why does the sender of the riddle apparently want *us* to find the secret?"

"That part is beyond me," Jean conceded. "But I'm sure someone besides the sender must know the secret. Perhaps whoever's been digging at the fountain wants to search underneath or cart it away to examine. Remember the chipping of the ice."

The girls concluded that if this surmise were right, whatever was buried under or inside the fountain had been there a long time. Why had it suddenly become an object of interest?

Louise and Jean continued to conjecture about the riddle. " 'What that is hidden is in plain sight?' "

Louise quoted. "If an object were in plain sight, surely it wouldn't be covered up."

The sisters went over every angle of the mystery. The only thing definite they could decide was that the Murrays and the person using the name Mrs. Stevenson did not want the fountain removed.

"Yet a Mr. Stevenson engaged a mason to remove it!" Jean pointed out.

To this enigma the girls could find no answer, though they were convinced that the blond masquerader must be one of the people hunting for whatever was hidden.

"I'd like to go to the Price homestead and look around again right away," said Jean as they entered their suite. "We might find another clue."

"With that ankle of yours?" Louise asked.

Jean made a face. "It won't hurt my ankle. Maybe Professor Crandall will drive us, then I wouldn't have far to walk."

Louise was about to consent to the plan, when a freshman, Alice Heady, knocked and announced, "Mrs. Crandall wants you both to come to the office at once. She also wishes Doris Harland, Evelyn Starr, and Lettie Briggs to be there."

Alice tapped on the doors of the other girls' rooms to inform them, then went downstairs. The group met in the hall. Doris and Evelyn wore puzzled looks, but Lettie seemed frightened.

"I know what Mrs. Crandall wants," she said. "Alice told me the police have sent for us!"

"Really?" Louise said in surprise.

Lettie began to whine. "I haven't done anything but play a few jokes! And you've done that yourselves!"

The other girls found it hard to suppress giggles. They were sure that the police did not want to question Lettie because of any pranks, but the four were thoroughly enjoying her discomfiture.

"You must have done something awful, Lettie," Jean needled.

"I—I haven't! I tell you everything was just in fun!" Lettie insisted.

Evelyn's eyes were twinkling. "That stolen riddle was probably a vital clue to the mystery."

"That was all in fun too," Lettie confessed.

By this time the five had entered Mrs. Crandall's office. She reiterated what Lettie had already told the girls and said she would give Louise permission to drive the school station wagon to headquarters. During the ride the girls chattered excitedly about why they had been summoned.

When they reached headquarters they found Captain James awaiting them. He ushered the girls into his private office, then requested the sergeant, "Bring in the prisoner."

When the man entered, he was introduced as Steve Lewyt. "Steve is a nickname—from stevedore," the officer explained.

The husky, muscular prisoner stood grim-faced and kept his eyes averted from the girls. The captain asked, "Do any of you recognize this man?"

The Starhurst group looked at him intently. They thought Lewyt seemed familiar but could not identify him.

"Maybe this will help you," the officer said, and turned to the sergeant. "Bring those things in."

A minute later the sergeant returned carrying a heavy jacket and a wig of long blond hair. The captain ordered them put on the prisoner.

Louise cried out, "Mrs. Stevenson!"

Lettie shrieked, "The—the woman who beat me up in the woods!"

"And threw the roadblock at me!" Jean cried out. Evelyn and Doris, as witnesses, corroborated this.

Louise had been looking at a ring on the little finger of the prisoner's right hand. Now she said, "I think Steve Lewyt is the person who sent Professor Crandall a threatening note! The ring on his finger could have made scratches like the ones on that paper."

The prisoner, livid with rage, tore off the wig and threw it across the room. Then he angrily removed the woman's coat.

"Okay, okay!" he snarled. "I did all those things!"

In the ensuing interrogation he confessed to having thrown the sandbag which had bruised Ken Scott's shoulder.

Doris spoke up angrily, "And you were the one who threw the snowballs. One had a stone in it that knocked me out!"

"And another contained a warning," Jean added.

"Yeah," Lewyt said. "You snooping girls got in my way too often. You didn't pay any attention to my warning, so I tried scaring you away with the gorilla costume like that other guy did. I saw you run. But don't think you're out of trouble yet, even if the cops have got me."

Louise asked him, "Did you chip ice off the fountain and fill the basin with water?"

"Yeah."

"Why?"

"I wanted to see them pretty figures on the fountain, so I brought a couple of pails, filled them with snow, and lighted a can of fuel. When the water was hot, I poured it on the figures. But it didn't do much good, so I started chipping. I guess it was the water that filled the basin."

Jean faced the prisoner and said, "One thing puzzled me. You warned us against removing the fountain. Why did you try to dig it up?"

Lewyt's eyes blazed. "I didn't! I wanted the fountain to stay right there."

"Just to *admire* it?" Louise spoke up skeptically.

"Sure, that's all."

Louise and Jean exchanged baffled glances. Lewyt sounded as if he were telling the truth about wishing the fountain to remain. Their guess that two factions were interested in the fountain must be true! It was not Lewyt but the other group which was trying to steal the fountain!

To satisfy herself on this point, Jean asked, "Weren't you the Mr. Stevenson who asked a mason to remove the fountain?"

"No. Positively no!"

The captain asked the girls if they had any more questions to put to the prisoner.

"I have," said Louise, then she asked Lewyt, "You started the avalanche off the roof that buried my sister and me?"

The prisoner did not reply, so she went on, "We found your boot marks by the dormer window on the third floor and a long, wet stick you must have used to shove the snow."

"Okay, I did it. You were getting too nosy."

Captain James asked Lewyt why and how he had entered the locked house. Suddenly the former stevedore began to laugh. "You cops are sure dumb you didn't figure that out. I wasn't the only one going into the house. Several times I found the front door unlocked and went inside to get out of the cold."

"And to steal valuable objects from the homestead," Louise accused him.

"What are you talking about?" the prisoner shouted. "There wasn't anything in that house."

The Danas thought, "The other faction are the

thieves!" Still, they felt that there was more to Lewyt's interest in the fountain than he had admitted.

Louise tried another tack. "Did you ever see anyone else except our group at the homestead?"

The prisoner gave a slight start. "N-no," he muttered hastily.

Lewyt denied knowing anything about the kidnapped men and said he had not been on the Price grounds at the time the two had disappeared. He could furnish a good alibi. "My landlady will tell you I was home that day from afternoon on."

Louise asked the captain how Lewyt had been apprehended. "I'll tell you as soon as he has been taken back to his cell," the officer answered.

After the sergeant had led the man away, the captain told the girls the policewoman had trapped Lewyt with the diamond which Louise had found in the fireplace. " 'Mrs. Stevenson' came to her house and asked where the stone had been found. She replied that it was near the homestead grounds."

The caller had at once insisted the gem was hers and for a small reward the policewoman had let "Mrs. Stevenson"—Steve Lewyt—take it.

"Plainclothes detectives shadowed his rented car to a boardinghouse where he'd taken a room," Captain James continued. "On the ride back he took off his disguise. At the house our detectives discovered a suitcase full of jewellery he had stolen from local stores. The thief admitted having removed the diamond from its setting.

"Also, they learned that Lewyt has a prison record as a jewel thief. During his last term he became pals with a prisoner serving a long sentence for the same thing. This pal once made a large haul of gems which has never been found. We believe he gave Lewyt some kind of a tip about the cache."

The officer smiled broadly. "Well, young ladies, thank you for coming down. All of you have been a great help."

The five girls left headquarters and rode back to the school. When Louise and Jean reached their suite, the two expressed a mutual worry.

"Jean," said Louise, "apparently Lewyt's the one who was keeping the fountain from being taken away. Without him around, the persons who have been digging it out can easily steal it now!"

"That's right," her sister agreed. "I think we should tell Professor Crandall everything immediately. It's almost dinnertime. Let's get ready quick and go see him."

The Danas had never changed clothes faster in their lives. Within minutes they were headed for the first floor. Professor Crandall himself answered their rap.

"Come in, come in," he said. "Tell us what happened at headquarters."

The full story was reported, then Jean said, "My

sister and I are fearful that with Lewyt in jail, the fountain will be stolen by this other group. Please, right after dinner, won't you take us girls and some strong men over there? We can drag the fountain away with ropes."

The elderly man considered this proposal. "You're right that we must lose no time," he agreed finally. "I will get our handy man and ask him to bring a couple of friends."

As soon as dinner was over, Louise and Jean hurried back upstairs to change into warm clothes. They met Professor Crandall at the school station wagon. A few minutes later the handy man and two husky companions appeared carrying large coils of rope. Professor Crandall said, "We will park a little distance from the homestead and proceed through the grounds on foot to the fountain."

Accordingly, he stopped the car about two hundred feet from the front walk. The group got out, turned on flashlights, and made their way into the grounds.

Louise and Jean were in the lead. In a few minutes they reached the garden. The two trained their flashlights toward the fountain, then gasped.

"It's gone!" Jean cried out.

CHAPTER XIX

Girl Deputies

A HEARTBROKEN cry came from Professor Crandall. "Oh, no! It can't be gone!" He stared at the empty spot where the beautiful fountain had stood.

For a moment the Danas were speechless, then the girls realized the group must act at once.

Louise swung her light around the grounds and said, "The fountain was dragged away. See these tracks? Let's follow them!"

This was easy to do because the marks in the snow were wide and deep. They led toward the street.

Jean's ankle, which was hurting a bit, kept her from hurrying. Her sister, ahead of the others, made a dash for the street. When Louise reached it, she looked first to the left, then to the right. Starhurst's handy man caught up to Louise. As he did, she exclaimed:

"I see the fountain! In that truck down there!"

The handy man peered to the right and saw an open pickup truck at the kerb. In back lay the Cellini fountain, over which a man was throwing a canvas. The next instant he jumped down, scrambled into the cab beside the driver, and the truck sped off.

At that moment Jean and the other men came up. Quickly Louise told the story. "We must follow them!"

The professor demurred. "I cannot let you girls run into danger," he said.

"But we can't let those thieves steal the fountain!" Jean argued.

The debate ended suddenly as a police station wagon drove up. McGuire and Kane were in it.

"The fountain has just been stolen!" Louise pointed at the retreating truck.

The two officers looked, and Officer McGuire said, "All of you jump in and we'll chase those men!"

The pursuit led far out into the country. McGuire, who was driving, radioed headquarters and asked for reinforcements. He was already beyond the town limits, but was told by the captain to continue the chase and at least find out the destination of the truck.

McGuire received further instructions that he was to keep the truck in sight but not overtake it.

The police captain thought it might be going to the spot where the kidnapped men were being held.

Presently they saw the truck turn down a side road. It was little more than a lane, and led to an abandoned, tumble-down farmhouse.

"That looks like a place from which the kidnapper-thieves might operate," Professor Crandall remarked.

"Right," Officer McGuire agreed, and pulled to a stop beyond the lane. "I think we'd better follow on foot." Quickly he contacted headquarters and gave their location.

Jean was already opening the door, ready to jump out. Professor Crandall said, "I don't feel able to go, so I will remain here. Don't you girls think you had better stay here too?"

The Danas' hearts sank. They wanted to see the next act of the exciting drama, yet they did not feel they could ignore the professor's request. Louise, however, looked appealingly at Officer McGuire.

Apparently he understood and said, "Professor Crandall, if I promise to see that no harm comes to these young ladies, will you put them in my care?"

The professor considered the suggestion for a moment. Finally he smiled. "I realize how Louise and Jean feel. But please, Officer, don't give them any dangerous assignment."

"I promise," said McGuire, getting out of the car.

He directed that the officers go first, then the girls, with the Starhurst handy man and his friends bringing up the rear.

The walk down to the abandoned farmhouse was about a quarter of a mile. It was evident that the place had not been occupied for some time and was in a bad state of disrepair. Barn and sheds were in even worse condition.

There were many lights on in the house, and as the group approached, they could hear loud, angry men's voices through a broken windowpane. The pickup truck was parked nearby, its engine still running. The men in the truck had not gotten out.

Officer McGuire halted his group a little distance from the spot and issued orders. "I am deputizing each of you for this job." As Louise and Jean looked surprised, he added, "Yes, you girls, too!"

Deputized! The Danas were so proud they could hardly keep from shouting.

"Now this is what I want you all to do," Officer McGuire went on. "You girls stay here and watch the fountain. If anyone takes it out, watch where it goes." With a wink he added teasingly, "If you have a chance to take the fountain away from the thieves, I know you'll do it."

"Oh, yes." The girls grinned excitedly.

It was arranged that the five men would surround all the buildings and make a search. "Perhaps we will find the kidnapped mason and trucker," said McGuire.

Officer Kane spoke up. "Everybody keep alert. Be ready for instant action if anyone comes out of the house."

The police and their men deputies took circuitous routes through a patch of woods to stay out of sight. The Danas, hidden behind a clump of brush, saw the two men in the truck get out and stand alongside it talking. The sisters strained their ears to hear.

"What are we goin' to do with this fountain?" one man asked impatiently.

"Nothin'," said the other. "We'll leave it for the boss."

The first man complained that he was hungry. "Let's go in the house and get somethin' to eat. I'm starved."

"But what if Red comes?" the second man asked. "He told us not to leave the fountain unguarded."

His companion scoffed. "Who's going to find it? Nobody!" He laughed smugly. "The police have been huntin' for us a long time and haven't thought of this place. Anyhow, Red won't be here for hours. He and the missus want to go skating again. They're a couple of nuts to take such chances."

"They sure are," the other man said. "Okay, let's go!"

Louise and Jean grabbed each other. So Red,

undoubtedly Red Shanley, was head of the gang of thieves! How long would it be, though, before he might show up?

His two henchmen walked over to the house and went inside. Louise and Jean conferred in whispers. "Our instructions from Officer McGuire were for us to take the fountain away if we had a chance," Jean reminded her sister with a chuckle.

Louise's eyes sparkled with excitement. "Jean," she said, "I'm going to try driving that truck! Then we'll have both the fountain and the truck as evidence."

"Great idea!" Jean agreed. "And if we can get back to Starhurst soon enough, we may be able to capture those phantom skaters! I'm sure they're Red Shanley and his wife."

"I am too."

Cautiously the two girls crept from hiding and got into the cab of the truck. Before touching anything, Louise examined the starter, the gears, the lights, accelerator, and brakes carefully. Sure now that she could manage to drive the truck, Louise started the engine. She backed around quickly, then headed down the lane toward the road.

"You did it!" Jean exclaimed. She leaned out her window and reported that men were rushing from the house. "Louise, they're running right into the arms of the police!"

In a moment the exciting scene was left behind as Louise raced down the lane to the highway. Suddenly she braked to a stop. A police car had turned in, and stopped also. The two state troopers inside were astounded to see the girls. "What's going on?" one shouted.

Louise called to them, "The police at the farmhouse need help. We have the fountain!"

Without further ado, the police car shot up the lane. Professor Crandall had hurried from the Penfield police station wagon. Almost speechless, he squeezed into the truck beside the Danas, saying he was delighted to have the fountain finally in his possession!

"But this is a w-wild ride!" he exclaimed, holding on to Jean's arm with one hand and the dashboard with the other. "I don't know what my wife will say to all this. It's most unladylike for you girls. And what w-will the townspeople think!"

Jean giggled and patted his arm. "Don't worry," she said soothingly. "Louise and I have been deputized by the police."

"What!" cried the professor. The sisters brought him up to date on the story. Louise, enjoying his reaction, said, "We have another surprise. Jean and I plan to capture Red Shanley!"

This was almost too much for Professor Crandall. Again, he begged the girls to take no chances. Jean said, "We won't." And Louise added, "In fact, I think you should ask the faculty, especially the men, to help us."

The elderly professor clasped and unclasped his

hands. Finally he said, "You had better take up your plan with my wife."

By this time they had reached the Price homestead and stopped so that the professor could pick up the school's station wagon. When they arrived at Starhurst, the headmistress was overwhelmed to hear of the evening's adventure. She congratulated the Danas upon recovering the fountain.

"I do hope," she said, "that now everything will settle down and we'll have some peace and quiet!"

"Our work isn't finished!" Jean spoke up. "And we think we can capture the ringleader of the thieves."

A perplexed, anxious look came into Mrs. Crandall's eyes. "Please explain," she requested.

Louise told of the girls' hunch that the phantom skaters were the wanted forger, Red Shanley, and his wife, and explained the plan for trapping them on the pond if they showed up there.

"I suggest that Jean and I wait upstairs and watch the pond. Members of the faculty can remain in the living room until we give the signal to capture them. If the skaters don't come by midnight, we'll give up."

Mrs. Crandall frowned. "Why don't we let the police take care of this?"

"Many of them," Jean answered, "are busy rounding up other members of the gang and searching for the kidnapped men."

"Besides," her sister added, "we could be wrong

about the skaters coming here, and I'd hate to send the authorities on a wild-goose chase."

"That sounds sensible," Mrs. Crandall conceded. "I dislike being mixed up in anything to do with criminals, but I suppose as good Americans we should do our part in helping capture them. So I will go along with your plan, girls."

"Oh, thank you!" Jean said. "Will you call the faculty members together?" Mrs. Crandall promised to do so.

The headmistress later said that she was very proud of her teaching staff. She had had a unanimous response—each of them was eager to help solve the mystery. As the men and women waited in the darkened living room, Louise and Jean looked from a rear window onto the school pond. It was a clear night. The rising moon made it light enough for skaters to perform without further illumination.

Minutes ticked by. Finally it was eleven-thirty. Louise and Jean, wearied from their exciting day, began to feel very drowsy. Nevertheless, they remained on guard.

Suddenly Louise jerked up straight from a slumped position. "There they are!" she exclaimed. "They just came out of the woods!"

Dressed in the same white, eerie costumes, the pair started off around the pond.

"Let's go!" Jean urged.

The two girls hurried downstairs and informed

those in the living room. It had been prearranged that should their services be needed, the teachers would surround the pond, and at a signal, converge on the Shanleys.

They and the Danas slipped noiselessly outside and separated. When the group had encircled the pond without being seen by the skaters, Mr. Norton, the athletic director, blew a whistle. At this very second Louise got a good look at the skating pair. She gasped.

"The man's not Red Shanley!" she thought. "That couple are Mr. and Mrs. Murray!"

It was too late for her to give any warning. The faculty members were rushing onto the ice. A moment later the Murrays were grabbed tightly and held!

CHAPTER XX

The Unknown Benefactor

MR. and Mrs. Murray fought like tigers. They pulled off their gloves and clawed at their captors.

The Danas rushed up. It suddenly occurred to them that if the couple were innocent of wrong-doing, why did they not say so? As the girls were thinking this, Mr. Murray's skating cap suddenly fell off.

He had red hair!

"His hair was black when we met him!" Louise gasped.

"You're Red Shanley!" Jean cried out. And Louise added, "You wore a dark wig when you came here to see Professor Crandall."

Before the couple had a chance to make any excuses, the policemen who had been summoned by Mrs. Crandall arrived.

The Stanleys were ordered to remove their skates, and march to the school's living room.

Under the bright light, with everyone crowding around, the red-haired man suddenly found his voice. "You have no right to hold me!" he rasped. "I have done nothing! And my wife is innocent too."

Professor Crandall spoke up. "Perhaps you will be amazed to learn that the fountain which you had your men steal is now safe here at Starhurst. The police have captured your gang."

"It can't be true!" cried Mrs. Shanley.

Mrs. Crandall proudly told of the Dana girls' part in tracing the fountain, and with police help, recovering it. As she was speaking, the telephone rang in her adjoining apartment. The headmistress hurried to answer, then came back smiling.

"The kidnapped men, Mr. Mareno and his friend, were found unharmed in the old farmhouse," she reported. "The criminals are all in custody."

The Danas and their teachers cheered. Mr. and Mrs. Shanley looked fearful and shifted uncomfortably.

The headmistress went on to say that the two men had been held captive not only to prevent them from removing the fountain, but also because of the incriminating evidence against Shanley and his gang which Mr. Mareno and his friend had overheard.

At this point, one of the police officers asked the

prisoners, "Do you wish to make a statement here or wait until we get to headquarters?"

The couple did not reply immediately, but finally Red Shanley shrugged and said, "I guess you've got the goods on me, so it doesn't matter. I've been known as a forger, and through my ability in that line I was hired by an international theft ring. The members steal art objects, including valuable fountains."

Louise asked him, "Then it was you who took costly art objects which had been left in the Price homestead?"

"Yes. I sold them to Biggers' Art Shop in New York."

Professor Crandall spoke up. "How did you—er—work your racket?"

Mrs. Shanley gave the answer. "One of our methods was to make a small down payment on a house which we knew contained something worth stealing. We did this in order to have free access to the grounds and not be suspected if we were seen inside the house."

Through further questioning it was learned that the Shanleys' primary interest had been the Cellini fountain. They had seen the valuable objects in the homestead when Mr. Black had shown them through the house.

Red Shanley looked balefully at the Danas. "I never thought I'd be caught by a couple of school girls," he said. "The first time you came to the Price homestead I was starting to carry away the last piece—a marble bust. When I heard you two downstairs, I dropped it."

"You hitchhiked a ride in the market truck that hit the school station wagon," Jean put in.

The man admitted this, saying he was on his way to the homestead. Later, with the help of wigs as a disguise he kept from being recognized and picked up by the Penfield police.

Jean asked the Shanleys if either of them had found a diamond at the homestead, then lost it.

Red's wife confessed that she had. "I put the diamond in my sweater pocket, and figured it must have dropped out, but I had no idea where." The woman was amazed to learn that the gem had been found in the fireplace ashes and that it had been stolen from a jewelry store.

"And you also dropped a white scarf near the pond," Jean remarked.

"So that's what happened to it," Mrs. Shanley said.

"What do the initials B. C. stand for?" Louise asked her.

Mrs. Shanley hesitated, then said, "My sister in New York City sent me the scarf. Maybe the shop put the B. C. on it."

"Didn't it ever occur to you that B. C. could stand for Benvenuto Cellini?"

The skater shook her head and suddenly the

onlookers could detect tears in her eyes. She said, "My sister is a lovely person. It shocked her when I married a man with a prison record. Ever since that time she has used secret methods to warn me not to be involved with his schemes. Maybe the initialled scarf was one of her warnings."

Louise and Jean were amazed at this unexpected angle, and immediately other pieces of the strange puzzle began to fall into place. Jean asked Mrs. Shanley, "Did your sister give an anonymous tip to the police that certain wanted criminals were on their way to Chicago?"

Red glared as his wife nodded. Then Louise asked her, "Did your sister send us Danas a riddle signed with the initials B. C.?"

"I don't know. She didn't tell me. Poor Margie! She tried so hard to keep Red and me out of trouble."

"Mrs. Shanley," said Louise, "do you know a man named Steve Lewyt?"

The woman prisoner was thunderstruck. In a weak voice she said, "Yes. He's my half-brother."

Jean spoke up. "Have you heard that Lewyt is in the local jail?"

"Oh, no!" Mrs. Shanley said. "I can't bear any more!" She looked as if she were about to faint. Mr. Norton dashed into the Crandall apartment and brought her a glass of cold water.

An angry look came over Red Shanley's face. "That fool brother-in-law of mine and I don't get along. He used to be part of our gang, but didn't cooperate. He heard about the Cellini fountain from a different source. I wanted it taken away and he wanted it to stay. I don't know why—he wouldn't tell me. My wife thought maybe her sister had talked him into going straight. Anyway, he was using the name Stevenson. I decided to try it myself to throw suspicion off my wife and me."

The Dana girls did not comment and Shanley went on, "Steve showed up here all of a sudden and made a lot of trouble for us. We would've had that fountain out of the place long ago if it hadn't been for him. We had a fight and I told him to get out of town. When he didn't show up today, I thought he had."

The two policemen ended the interrogation by handcuffing the prisoners and leading them away.

After they had gone, Mrs. Crandall served cocoa and cookies to the faculty and the Danas. Praise was high for the two girls, but as they were getting ready for bed a short time later, Louise remarked to Jean, "Do you realize that we haven't yet solved the riddle of the fountain?"

"I realize it all right. I think Steve Lewyt was telling the truth about why he chipped the ice. But since he didn't unearth any treasure despite his digging, I think the answer lies right in the fountain itself."

Her sister agreed. "Let's get up real early so we can take a closer look at the fountain."

Next morning, they dressed warmly and went to see the handy man. He and his helpers moved the beautiful piece into the school's large cellar. They were extremely careful not to damage the exquisite dancing nymphs.

The fountain was set upright in the hot furnace room. The ice on it began to melt even before the Danas had removed their outdoor wraps.

This gave Louise an idea. "Maybe that treasure isn't hidden *inside* the statue, but under the ice in the basin. Let's chip it away and find out!"

Aided by the heat from the furnace and several tools, the girls did not find the job too hard. As Jean lifted out a large chunk of ice, she suddenly exclaimed, "Louise, look!"

Clinging to the bottom of the chunk were several diamonds!

Excitedly the girls went on chipping away the rapidly melting ice. In a few minutes they had uncovered a fortune in loose gems lying on the bottom of the basin! Leaves and the debris of years had covered them over, then the water had frozen, making an excellent hiding place for the precious stones.

"This must be the 'loot' hidden by Steve Lewyt's prison pal!" Louise said. "He must have thrown it here in a hurry."

Quickly the girls gathered up the gleaming gems and put them into a paper bag which was lying on a shelf in the furnace room.

"We must show these to the Crandalls immediately," said Louise, "and then take them to police headquarters."

A little later, when the diamonds were emptied onto Mrs. Crandall's desk, she stared in amazement, and summoned her husband. After hearing the Danas' story, the professor exclaimed, "So this treasure was the mystery surrounding the frozen fountain!"

The sisters received permission to drive to headquarters directly after breakfast and deliver the diamonds. Captain James was astonished and said, "It won't be hard to find the owner of these jewels. The record of Lewyt's prison pal should give the answer."

"May we speak to Lewyt?" Louise requested. "I have a question I'd like to ask him."

The captain nodded, and a sergeant accompanied the Danas to the cellblock. Lewyt was astounded to learn that the diamonds he had hoped to locate himself had been found by the girls.

"I was pretty dumb not to think of looking under the leaves and ice. My friend only mentioned a valuable fountain around here. He should have told me exactly where he put the stuff."

The Danas smiled at this remark—did any criminal trust another criminal?

"We'd like to ask you something," said Louise. She first explained what they had learned of the Shanleys, then about the riddle and how it had been a valuable clue in their solving the fountain mystery. Now she said, "Steve, do you think your half-sister in New York might have sent the riddle?"

The prisoner frowned. "Could be. I heard about you girls when I first came here, and mentioned you to her. I said I'd better watch my step with you around. Margie is always trying to keep me from stealing, so maybe she sent the riddle to you so you'd figure it out and keep me from prison. I'd told her I was going to look for a treasure near the fountain. That's why I didn't want it moved and tried to scare everybody away. Let me see that riddle."

Jean said, "We don't have it with us."

"Well, I'll tell you how you can identify the typewriter Margie uses. The *i*'s are blurred."

Further questioning of the prisoner by the sisters corroborated the Shanleys' story. Lewyt had come to the homestead on his own, and had been astounded to find the Shanleys there. "I tried to get 'em away, but they wouldn't budge," Lewyt complained.

The Danas thanked him for the information and went off. They were curious about the writer of the riddle who evidently wanted to be a benefactor!

"At least," Jean reflected, "she's trying to reform two members of her family, and also give you and me clues to find the diamonds and help the police restore the stolen diamonds to their rightful owner."

"I'd certainly like to see that paper again," said Louise.

"We haven't had any luck getting it back," Jean replied. "Maybe if Professor Crandall makes a plea, the guilty person will hand it over."

The professor was very happy to cooperate and during luncheon called for attention. He first mentioned the fact that through the riddle the Danas had been able to find a cache of stolen diamonds which would be given back to their owner. "The person who took the riddle from Louise Dana will do the school and the police department a great favour by returning it."

He paused and looked intently around the dining room. Then Professor Crandall said, "I have another important announcement to make, thanks to Evelyn Starr. Just this morning she found the missing half of an old map of the Starhurst grounds on which a spring is marked. Less than an hour ago it was opened up. Now the Cellini bronze fountain can soon be set in place to help beautify our campus."

All the students clapped loudly and called for Evelyn to stand up and take a bow. Then they asked for Louise and Jean, who graciously acknowledged the ovation.

When the Danas returned to their room, they found the missing paper with the riddle on it lying upon Louise's desk. They bent over and looked at it carefully. Every *i* was fuzzy!

"Now we know definitely who composed and sent the riddle," said Louise. "And that's the last of the mysteries."

She said this wistfully, and both sisters felt a sense of loss without a case to work on! But they were soon to find themselves in the midst of another baffling mystery, which came to be known as *The Secret of the Silver Dolphin*.

A few days later the bronze fountain stood in its new home. When the Starhurst students and faculty were gathered around it, the water was turned on and began to run down freely over the graceful dancing nymphs.

"Oh, it's beautiful—perfectly beautiful!" Doris exclaimed.

Everyone agreed and all the students joined in singing their alma mater song. Louise and Jean were thrilled with the outcome of their work on the mystery. First thing the next morning the sisters hopped from bed, went to the window, and looked out at the beautiful fountain. The water was not flowing any longer. Instead, the fountain was covered with ice.

Louise smiled. "It looks more natural that way."

"Yes," said Jean, putting an arm around her sister. "And it will be a reminder until spring of our adventures solving the riddle of the frozen fountain!"